I0563414

# Horn of Plenty

Martha Jane Hovater

Published by Arian Derwydd Books, LLC, 2024.

How does Mac Hollingsworth, a French Horn player in the Navy Band, become involved in a plot to deploy a bioweapon? Where did it come from? What is the intended target? And what can she possibly do to prevent its deployment?

Mac discovers something unusual one day while cleaning her horn and is suddenly "reassigned." A woman she doesn't know is killed while driving Mac's car. Someone keeps trying to kill her. And she finds herself working with people who are not who they seem.

This book is a work of fiction. Any resemblance to persons, living or dead, actual events, locale, or organizations is entirely coincidental.
Arian Derwydd Books, LLC
https://arianderwyddbooks.com/
Horn of Plenty
Copyright © 2024 by Martha Jane Hovater
ISBN: 979-8-9902245-0-6

# Acknowledgments

Since I was a child, I've written stories of various kinds and often thought of writing a novel. I started writing several, but I always allowed life to get in the way. I even completed a master's degree in English, but I never made writing a priority.

In late 2022, however, my oldest son, Mychael Johnson-Cook, and I made an accountability pact to write every Sunday and share what we had written in a phone call. Myc has been a prolific writer (under various names) for many years. A couple of years ago, he even established his own publishing company (Arian Derwydd Books). Given his list of published work, I think it's unlikely that Myc needed our accountability pact as much as I did, but we have kept that pact with each other ever since. That commitment to writing every week continued for me and grew into a commitment to writing at other times, too. That commitment was the reason I was finally able to achieve a lifelong goal of writing a novel, and I am deeply grateful to him for helping me do that.

Now, however, Myc is not only my son and "writing buddy," but also my editor and publisher, and his efforts in those roles have been both encouraging and priceless! Thank you, Myc—for everything.

I also deeply appreciate the work of Nadia Biddle for proofreading the completed manuscript.

In addition to being a writer (of one kind or another) for most of my life, I was also a French Horn player. I had to give up playing several years ago, but I'm still very much a horn lover and a 'horn person' (a concept that perhaps only other horn players may understand). I used my love of the French Horn to develop the character, MacKenzie Hollingsworth, and

I am certain she (and other characters from *Horn of Plenty*) will appear again in another novel or two!

So—I knew a few things about writing, and I knew a few things about the French Horn, but I knew almost nothing about the military (and Internet research is often not enough). Consequently, I was grateful that Chief Musician Jason Ayoub, Principal Horn of the United States Navy Concert Band; and Musician 1st Class April Enos, U.S. Navy Band Public Affairs, took time from their very busy schedules to answer several questions that made some of the details in *Horn of Plenty* more accurate. Thank you again, Jason and April for your help and your service to the Navy Band and our country!

And last, but definitely not least, I thank my life partner, Barbara White, for her love, her support, for listening to me read every Sunday, and for her patience with a very long process.

*I dedicate this book to the 5th-grade girl who wrote a story about a wonderful dragon.*

# Chapter 1

It wasn't the proverbial 'dark and stormy night.' If it had been, it might have been easier to understand why the car Annie Headley was driving was damaged beyond recognition. Annie did not survive, so any explanation of what happened was lost with her, at least until an investigation was complete.

The common, often well-intended expression "everything happens for a reason" is usually a platitude uttered as a suggestion of some divine or existential purpose. Still, it was often true on a more earthly, human level. That was the case with Annie's death. Annie died because she was driving Mac Hollingsworth's car and because at least in the fading light. she bore a slight resemblance to her—someone she didn't even know.

MacKenzie Hollingsworth was just getting out of the shower when her phone rang. She answered it with her right hand as she continued to towel off her hair with her left. She didn't recognize the number.

"Hello?"

"Hello," a deep male voice responded. "I'm trying to reach MacKenzie Hollingsworth."

"Well, you found her. And this is?"

"Maryland State Police, ma'am. I'm afraid there's been an accident."

"What kind of accident?" Mac asked as she stopped drying her hair and thoughts of her sister ran through her mind.

"It would probably be better if you came down to the station, ma'am," the officer responded. "Ask for Captain Vick when you arrive."

Mac was polite, but firm. "I'm not going anywhere until you tell me what this is about. Is this about my sister? Did McKenna have an accident?"

Captain Vick hesitated a moment, then said, "It's about Ann Headley, ma'am."

"Who's Ann Headley?" Mac asked as concern gave way to confusion.

"You don't know an Ann Headley?" Officer Vick asked.

"No, I don't, so I don't understand..."

"Ann Headley was killed in an automobile accident last night."

Mac remained confused. "I'm sorry to hear that, Captain, but I don't understand why you're calling me."

"I'm calling you, ma'am, because the car Ms. Headley was driving was registered in your name."

Mac sat down on the end of the bed, stunned, but then she began grabbing clothes. "I'm on my way," she said and hung up. She used her speed dial for her next conversation. When her sister, McKenna, answered, she asked, "Who is Ann Headley, Kenna, and why the hell was she driving my car?"

"How did you..." McKenna began.

"Maryland State Police just called me, Kenna. They said she was killed in an accident last night—in my car."

"Oh, my God," McKenna gasped, then took a moment to catch her breath. "Oh, my God," she said again.

"Kenna?" Mac began.

McKenna choked back her tears. "Annie was a friend of mine, Mac. I..." she hesitated, "I let her borrow your car yesterday. It's a long story, Mac. I'm sorry. But right now, I'm more sorry about Annie."

"Okay," Mac said, aware of McKenna's shock and grief. "We'll talk later. Right now, I'm going to the police station." Mac started to say goodbye, but then added, "You know, Kenna, you should probably come with me. How about I pick you up in a half hour?"

"Yeah, okay," McKenna managed.

Mac threw on the rest of her clothes and hurried out the door of her apartment. She climbed into her rental car and began the drive to her sister's home. She was annoyed that McKenna had loaned out her car without her permission. Then again, she had been nice enough to keep it at her home while Mac had been away—but that was all over now, sort of. Recently, after fifteen years of service, she learned she was suddenly no longer Principal French Horn in the United States Navy Concert Band. Well, maybe she was and maybe she wasn't. It was a strange situation and an even stranger feeling.

Mac pulled into the familiar driveway and saw her sister waiting for her on the front porch. McKenna walked to the car and got in.

"Hi, Mac," she said. "I'm sorry I didn't..." Her voice broke, and tears threatened again.

Mac sighed. "Look, Kenna," she began, "I'm not happy about the situation, but what's done is done. Now we've got to deal with the fact that your friend is gone."

McKenna nodded. "Yeah, I know. I just never imagined something like this would happen, but then no one ever does, I guess. That's why they're called accidents, right?"

"Sure, Kenna," Mac replied as she backed out of the driveway, "but I'm still sorry about your friend."

"Thanks. She was a good friend. She was there for me when I was going through the divorce last year. I don't know what I would have done without her."

"Tell me about her."

McKenna sighed. "Well, Annie has been having some problems of her own recently, and I've tried to be there for her the same way she was for me. Her ex was giving her a hard time about visitation with the kids. They were beginning to work things out, but he called her yesterday to say that he couldn't bring them home because he was having car trouble. As it happens, Annie's car was in the shop having brakes installed, so I offered to loan her your car to go to New York and pick up the kids. I guess she was on her way there last night when the accident happened."

\* \* \*

Captain James Vick hung up the phone. He disliked giving people bad news, and he especially disliked doing it over the phone. The woman on the receiving end of the call had given him little choice, though. He was puzzled by her response. The accident victim, Ann Headley, appeared to be a law-abiding citizen without even a traffic ticket for over five years, so it was unlikely that she had suddenly decided to steal a car. Yet the car's owner didn't know her, and the car had not been reported stolen. Things didn't add up, but after ten years in the Maryland State Police, he had learned they usually did once all the pertinent facts were known. He decided to get a cup of coffee and look over his reports from the night before while he waited for MacKenzie Hollingsworth to arrive. It wasn't only the phone call that didn't make sense to him. The "accident" didn't make sense, either.

There had been no bad weather conditions, no heavy traffic in the area of the accident, no sharp curves or other dangerous road conditions, and even if there had been, the circumstances responsible for the accident were not clear. The car did not appear to crash into anything, and the lack of skid marks indicated that the driver had not struggled to control the vehicle. The car had exploded. He had seen the results of many car bombs during his tours of duty in Iraq, and this accident had all the markings of a similar event. Pieces of the vehicle were spread out in a radius of half a mile.

He wasn't sure how to explain that to the owner of the vehicle, but he knew he would have to tell her. Why would anyone want to blow up a model citizen like Ann Headley? Or was the explosion intended for the owner of the vehicle? He decided to do a little research on MacKenzie Hollingsworth as he sipped his coffee and waited for her arrival.

MacKenzie Hollingsworth also appeared to be a law-abiding citizen, and not only that, but she was also a member of the United States Navy. Or at least she had been. It appeared she had recently separated from the service. That was all the information he could find on her. The address on her vehicle registration was not current. Officers had gone to that address to make a notification of the accident, and no one there knew her. He did manage to find a phone number, which he had found through a friend at the Pentagon, and then used that number to contact her. His curiosity about her would not last long, however.

Vick's desk sergeant buzzed him. "There's a MacKenzie Hollingsworth here asking for you, sir."

"Thanks, Mike," he responded. "I'll be right up."

Captain Vick rose and headed down the hall to the front desk area. He wasn't sure what he had expected MacKenzie Hollingsworth to look like or be like, he just knew that whatever his expectation was, it bore no resemblance to reality. There were actually two women in the lobby area, but he knew almost immediately which one was Hollingsworth. She reminded him of Merida, in the Disney animated film, *Brave*. Her hair was a fiery red, curly, frizzy, and pulled back into a short ponytail. She stepped forward as he appeared in the doorway.

"MacKenzie Hollingsworth, Captain Vick," she said, extending her right hand in the expectation that he would shake it. He did so without thinking.

"Yes, ma'am," he replied, and then looked to the other woman with her.

"My sister, McKenna Hollingsworth," she said.

"Ma'am," he said, nodding to McKenna. "Would you both please follow me?" he asked as he turned down the hall. He led them to a small conference room halfway down the hall. "Please have a seat. Can I get either of you anything? Coffee, soft drink, water?"

"I appreciate your courtesy, Captain," Mac replied, "but I think we'd both prefer to learn exactly why we are here."

"What can you tell me about Ann Headley and how she came to be driving your car?"

The question was directed to Mac, but it was McKenna who answered. "Annie was a friend of mine. Mac's car was at my house, and I let Annie borrow it yesterday."

Vick's next question was a query for information, but it was also intended to get a reaction from one or both of them. "Do you know of anyone who might want Annie dead?"

McKenna gasped. "Oh, no! Of course not! Why would you ask such a thing?"

Captain Vick registered McKenna's shock, then turned to Mac, "Ma'am?"

Mac shook her head. "I can't help you there, Captain. I didn't know Ann Headley." She paused. "But your question implies this was not an accident."

Vick was tentative. "The investigation has just begun so nothing is definitive yet, but no, ma'am, I don't believe it was." He made his next statement as he made direct eye contact with Mac. "Your car exploded, ma'am." He paused for a moment before adding, "I'm wondering if you have any idea about why that happened."

Mac's eyes were still on Vick, but McKenna interrupted whatever thoughts were churning up between them.

"Oh, my God, Mac. I think I'm going to be sick."

Mac reached for the small trash can that was against the wall and handed it to her sister, who began throwing up.

Captain Vick pushed the intercom button on the phone. "We need some paper towels in Room 1," His gaze remained on Mac.

"You think the explosion was intended for me," she said.

Vick nodded. "Yes, ma'am, I think it was." He paused for a moment, then added, "Who might want *you* dead, Ms. Hollingsworth?"

* * *

The man behind the desk was livid. "It was supposed to look like an accident, you idiot," he hissed. "Now we'll have every three-letter agency in the country investigating this thing." He threw the iPad onto the desk after taking another glance at the video.

The assassin shrugged. "I don't know what happened. I rigged it to take out the brakes and steering when she reached sixty-five. Something went wrong."

"You think?" The man leaned back in his chair and closed his eyes. "Well, it's done. She's gone. We'll just have to make sure the investigation goes nowhere. For now, just go."

"Go where?"

The man opened his eyes and looked across the desk. "Go wherever it is that you go when you screw up." He waved him away with his hand. "I'll be in touch."

The errant assassin left the room, and once again, the man leaned back in his chair and closed his eyes.

"I'm sorry, Mac," he said out loud.

He had hoped he could avoid killing her—no, he had hoped he could avoid having her killed. He knew he couldn't do it himself. Part of him cared too much about her, but only part. He couldn't say he loved her. It wasn't like that. He wasn't sure exactly what it was, but it wasn't love. Friendship, maybe—but wasn't that a kind of love? He shook his head to clear those thoughts away. It was over now. He could move on without worrying about her getting in the way. Ever. He got up from his ornate desk and went to the bar. He poured himself a drink and clicked on the TV. He flipped through several channels of commercials before finding what he was looking for.

"Breaking news," the TV anchor said. "We've received unconfirmed reports of a possible car bomb that exploded just north of Baltimore. We've learned that there was one fatality, Ann Headley of Annapolis." Ann's picture was suddenly on the screen. "Stay tuned, and we will cover additional details as the story continues to develop."

The man stopped mid-sip of his twenty-year-old Scotch and closed his eyes again. Not only had the assassin bungled the bomb, but he had also killed the wrong person. Who the hell is Ann Headley? He reached for his phone, but it rang before he could dial the number that had just appeared on his caller ID.

"I'm afraid I have more bad news," the assassin said.

"I know. I just heard it on the news," the man responded. "What are we going to do about that?"

"I'll get her," the assassin responded, "and this time, it *will* look like an accident."

"Are you insane?" the man replied. "There will be an investigation, and they will figure out that Mac was the intended target. It will be almost impossible to get to her now."

"*Almost* impossible," repeated the assassin. "It will be difficult, yes, but not impossible."

\* \* \*

After several minutes of attending to McKenna, Mac looked up to see Captain Vick still eyeing her, his question still unanswered—and raising his eyebrows to nonverbally repeat it.

Mac shrugged. "I don't know what to tell you, Captain. I was just recently discharged from the Navy, and I've only been back home for a few days."

"Uh huh," Vick muttered. "And what exactly did you do in the Navy, Ms. Hollingsworth?"

"Please call me Mac—everybody does." She paused to check on McKenna again before meeting Vick's eyes—his eyebrows raising again.

"I'm a musician. I was a member of the Navy Concert Band."

"Musician... okay."

"I play the French Horn. It's the brass instrument with lots of curled tubing, "she said, making a curling motion with her hand.

"Uh huh," Vick muttered again. "I know what a French Horn is. I played baritone in my high school band."

"Cool," Mac said with a nod and a weak smile.

"So why would someone want a Navy French Horn player dead, *Mac*?" He emphasized his use of her nickname. "You hit a wrong note or something?"

Mac's weak smile faded. "Look, Captain." She nodded toward McKenna, who was no longer throwing up but looked pale and shaken. "My sister is sick, and her friend has been killed. Can we talk about this another time?"

Vick folded his arms and was thoughtful for a moment. "Okay." He nodded. "You and your sister can leave—with a couple of non-negotiable conditions."

"Such as?"

"One—you don't go home or to your sister's house. Two—I'm going to post a car wherever you decide to stay tonight."

"Just for tonight?"

"Maybe. Maybe longer."

"So you want us to find a hotel to hide out in for an indefinite period?" She shook her head. "We're not wealthy people, Captain."

"Okay, then I have an alternative suggestion," he offered. "There's a hotel not far from here. I suggest you spend the night there. The department keeps a room there. That way your names won't be registered."

"Your department keeps a room at a local hotel?" Mac asked incredulously.

"Yeah, we do. Let's get the two of you out of here."

# Chapter 2

The errant assassin sat in his hotel room, cleaning his weapons. He hadn't used any of them for a while, but it didn't matter. Cleaning his weapons was almost a daily ritual for him. It was a compulsion that began after his first *assignment* as a civilian.

He had learned the tools of his trade from the best of the best who lived and breathed to make him and his brothers the best of the best. Some of his brothers almost died in the process. But they all somehow survived Hell Week and were given the distinction of becoming Navy Seals.

He had served with honor for almost five years, proud to use what he had learned to defend his country and all that he cared about. All of that ended one night when he and his fiancé were hit head-on by a drunk driver. The driver had a few minor injuries but was able to walk away in handcuffs after police found that his blood alcohol level was three times the legal limit.

Jessica was killed, and he had several severe injuries, which resulted in him almost losing both legs, but the surgeon was able to save one of them. He saved the left leg by piecing it together with metal. He also had a severe concussion. In the years since the accident, he often thought of the irony that he had survived Afghanistan and Iraq with only a few minor injuries but was nearly killed by a fellow naval officer who turned to alcohol after his last deployment and returning home to learn that his wife was having an affair and wanted a divorce.

*That guy's wife left him, and he took away the love of my life permanently*, the assassin thought as he methodically moved through his weapon-cleaning ritual. *He also ended my career as a Navy Seal.*

He was aware that he was different now in many ways. Recovery had taken everything he had, and though he recovered well physically, he knew his thought process was very different. However, he didn't talk to anyone about those things.

* * *

The man behind the desk threw his Sat phone across the room. *Idiot*, he thought. *He not only botched the hit. He killed the wrong person.*

The news report had said Ann Headley had two kids. The situation was not something he would have chosen, but it happened. Now two kids would grow up without a mother. Part of him felt sorry about that. Part of him felt numb and told himself they were collateral damage.

*Strange*, he thought, *how we can have such two different thoughts and feelings at the same time.*

He had conflicting feelings about Mac, too. He liked her a lot. She was smart, talented, and had been both a colleague and casual acquaintance. Part of him might have cared too much about her. Part of him realized she could now be a threat that had to be eliminated.

"No loose ends," they had said.

*Yeah, strange how the mind works.*

He crossed the room, picked up his Sat phone, and dialed the number. "Where the hell did you get this guy?" he asked the woman who answered the call.

"He came highly recommended," the woman said. There was no response. "Okay," the woman said, "he screwed up, but I think he'll take care of it."

"Take care of it?" the man yelled into the phone. "Right. He may take care of it but not without lots of eyes watching Mac now."

"Mac?" she asked. "You know her?"

The man was taken aback momentarily. "Yeah," he said with a sharper tone to his voice, "but that's none of your business, and it has no bearing on the business at hand." He abruptly ended the call and threw the Sat phone across the room again. "Damn it, Mac!" he yelled, even though no one was present to hear him.

\* \* \*

Captain Vick used a key card at the back door of the hotel. It was 1 A.M., and no one was in the parking lot or the hall. Vick introduced Mac and McKenna to a detective named George, who would keep watch until morning.

The hotel room was at the end of the hall, and two armchairs sat on opposite sides of the hall next to a large window facing another section of the parking lot. Even in the darkness, Mac had noticed George's salt-and-pepper hair. She subtly turned her head to Vick.

"Old guy, huh?" she asked, raising her eyebrows.

Vick smiled. "Yeah, like me," he said, running his hand through his graying hair, "but don't let that fool you. He's the best I've got, and he's solid as a rock." He nodded. "Don't worry. You and your sister are in good hands tonight."

McKenna walked to the second of two double beds in the room and sat down as Mac locked the door. McKenna had been silent on the ride to the hotel. She looked pale and a little shaky, but finally spoke.

"Why are we here, Mac?" She shook her head. "Annie is dead. They say your car exploded, and they seem to think you were supposed to be the target?" She turned her head toward her sister, eyebrows raised to emphasize the questions.

Mac took a bottle of water from the small refrigerator and handed it to McKenna. "Here," she said. "You're pale and shaky and probably dehydrated from all the vomiting."

McKenna opened the bottle and took a few sips. "Maybe I am a little dehydrated, but I'm also pale and shaky because my best friend was just killed by a car bomb that may have been meant for you."

Mac nodded. "I know," was all she said. She returned to the small refrigerator to get a bottle of water for herself. She sipped the water as she slowly moved around the room.

"What..."

Mac silenced her sister's question by putting a finger to her lips. She ran her fingers under the desk and stopped momentarily. She held up one finger and then continued her movement around the room. She stopped again after running her hand behind one of the bed headboards. She held up two fingers. McKenna didn't speak but looked puzzled.

Mac opened the desk drawer to see if it held any stationery, which it didn't. She glanced at McKenna and nodded toward her handbag, making a motion with her hands like she was writing. McKenna nodded and got out a small notebook and pen she used for grocery lists or other reminders.

Mac took the notebook and pen offered by her sister and began to write. She then handed the notebook back to McKenna, whose eyes widened as she read.

*I've found two listening devices here. There may be more. There may be other surveillance devices that are not easily detectable. We can't talk here—at least not about this situation.*

McKenna frowned and tossed the notebook on the bed before looking at Mac with her hand thrown up and mouthing. "WTF?"

Mac picked up the notebook and wrote again.

*I'll tell you what I can when we're able to talk privately. For now, we need to limit our conversation to Ann and family stuff.*

McKenna read Mac's response and slowly put the notebook on the bed, frowning at her sister but nodding her understanding.

\* \* \*

"Damn!" Captain Vick pulled off his headset and threw it on the table, then turned to the audio technician. "Keep recording. Maybe we'll get lucky." He walked down the hall to his office and closed the door, pondering which private number to call on his burn phone.

Vick had friends at various agencies whom he had served with in the Marine Corps years before. After weighing his options, he called the friend who was the closest thing he had to a brother.

"Hey," he said, when his friend, Steve, answered.

"Hey back, man. What's up?" Steve asked, knowing Vick only used the burn phone when he needed to discuss a professional—and often questionable—issue. Steve had the same practice.

Vick sighed. "I've got a new case, and my gut's telling me there's more to it than may appear on the surface."

"Yeah, well, your gut's usually right about things like that. Tell me what you need to know."

Vick knew Steve wouldn't be on his cell phone at work, so he was cautious. "You're not in the office today?"

"Nah, I'm off today. I'm in my cage, man, you know, doing stuff."

Vick knew Steve had a Faraday cage in an outbuilding in his backyard. He also knew that 'doing stuff' could mean anything from playing an online game to hacking into supposedly secure websites. He wasn't sure how Steve was using his cell phone in the cage, but he decided not to ask for details. He gave his friend an overview of all that had happened in the last forty-eight hours.

"I've got Hollingsworth and her sister in protective custody at the moment, but there are too many things that just don't add up."

Vick heard his friend clicking keys on his computer. "Hollingsworth... Navy Band, huh?" Steve muttered as he continued clicking.

"That's the story." Vick sighed, his frustration growing.

"I get your frustration, brother. Hang on, I'm still poking around."

There was silence between them for close to thirty seconds before Vick's curiosity won out.

"Steve?"

"Yeah," Steve said slowly. "I'm still here. I... wait a second."

There was another long pause.

"Well," Steve began slowly. "She was a French Horn player in the Navy Concert Band. Wound up serving fifteen years before she left recently." Steve paused for another long moment. "I guess that's the good news. She was straight with you about that."

"I'm guessing you're about to tell me there's also bad news."

"You guessed right, man. The file I'm looking at is a Navy file, but there's an attached file that I can't open."

"A file *you* can't open? I never heard that one before."

"Yeah, I know, right? The thing is it's one of those files that will set off a bunch of alarm bells if I try," Steve explained. "But I've seen files like this before, and it makes me think she might be one of us."

"She's NSA?" Vick gasped.

"I'm not positive, man, but that's my hunch. Look, Vick, I can't touch this."

"Yeah, I know, I know. I don't want this to come back to bite you."

"Yeah, I appreciate that," Steve responded. "But listen, Vernon Jordan's name is somehow connected to this. You've worked with him some, haven't you? Why not ask him about it?"

Vernon Jordan was the head of Section 5 at NSA, and Vick *had* worked with him on occasion.

"Jordan, huh?" Vick was thoughtful. "That's helpful information, Steve, thanks. Maybe I'll do that."

Vick disconnected the call and leaned back in his chair. He knew Jordan was working on something top secret, but he'd heard nothing more. Hollingsworth had been in the Navy

Band, was now somehow involved with the NSA, and Vernon Jordan was connected. Interesting, indeed.

Vick rose from his desk when his regular cell phone buzzed. He answered it as he started down the hall back toward the audio lab. "Captain Vick here."

"Hi, Vick. I know it's been a while. This is Vernon Jordan."

Vick was not prone to anxiety, but he suddenly felt a twinge of it, wondering if Steve's Faraday cage was as secure as it was supposed to be. He pushed down the anxiety to respond without Jordan picking up on it.

"Jordan. Good to hear from you anytime. What can I do for you?"

"I just learned that you have an NSA person of interest in protective custody—MacKenzie Hollingsworth."

"Hollingsworth? Yeah, I've got her in protective custody along with her sister. Someone blew up her car. We haven't even really begun the investigation yet."

Jordan paused for a moment before saying, "Vick, you're still on the books with NSA, so I'm counting on your help here."

"What do you need?"

"I need for the Maryland State Police to forget about this case. We're assuming jurisdiction, and I'd like for you to facilitate that."

Vick smiled and responded, "Sure, Jordan, I think I've built a rapport with her already. I'll take good care of her and keep you informed."

"Very good," Jordan said. "Use this number to reach me. And thanks for your help."

"Glad to do it," Vick replied as they both ended the call. Vick didn't believe in coincidences, but this seemed to be one. Or was it?

*  *  *

George Gordon settled in his chair, radio in hand, gun under his jacket, and readied himself for a long night. His partner, Leo Mason, was outside in an unmarked car and would relieve George in a few hours so he could eat and use the bathroom, which George was finding a more frequent need as he got older. A uniformed officer would rotate out with Leo as needed. It was a good plan—one they'd used multiple times without incident. After tonight, however, that would no longer be true.

George dutifully monitored activity in the hall and through the large window. It was 2 A.M., and there wasn't much to see. The only other people he saw were a couple who seemed to be returning to their room after some kind of formal affair and a man in jeans and a black, hooded Baltimore Ravens sweatshirt, carrying a McDonald's bag and sipping on some kind of soft drink. He seemed to walk with a slight limp as he made his way down the crossing hallway.

George waited a few minutes before taking a few steps to peek around the corner. The hall was clear. *McDonald's at 2 A.M.*, he thought, shaking his head, *my stomach could never handle that.* He was a little hungry, though, and decided he'd settle for a granola bar he had in his pocket. It would go well with the cup of coffee still waiting for him on the windowsill if it wasn't already cold. Seeing no one and hearing no one, he turned to go back to his seat at the window and felt a sudden pinch in the back of his neck. In the few seconds between falling to the floor and losing consciousness, he thought he saw a Baltimore Ravens sweatshirt.

George was a big man, but so was his assailant, who was also younger and stronger. He hauled George the short distance to the seat by the window and managed to pull him up onto the seat, leaning his head against the window. Then he headed back to the crossing hall where he pulled a fire alarm before moving back outside the door to Mac and McKenna's room and waited.

* * *

The man behind the desk stood up and stretched. It felt good. He'd been sitting behind the desk for a long time, sorting through various files on his laptop. He looked around his well-appointed home and realized it wasn't just in the past few days he'd been sitting too long. He'd been sitting there for weeks, monitoring data on his laptop and keeping tabs on various things with his secure phone always within reach.

After stretching his back and arms, he began walking around the room. There were a few books on the shelves representing a variety of genres—leatherbound and looking more like part of the décor than books that had been read and loved. There were a few quite expensive works of art. They were investments but were also pieces he enjoyed seeing.

There were no photographs. In fact, there was nothing of a personal nature. He kept what few personal items he had in another location, a storage room he rarely visited anymore.

He had made choices—hard choices that meant giving up something he loved—something he missed. He was compensated well for the work he had done, and for several years, he believed he could have both financial and personal satisfaction in the double life he was living. However, a few weeks ago, things had gotten out of hand in many ways. He had plenty of money—maybe even enough to disappear. The money was the easy part. Disappearing was the hard part—at least disappearing and staying alive. He knew that if things weren't settled soon, there were important people who would make sure he disappeared permanently.

He went back to his desk, picked up his laptop, and placed it on one of the side tables between two expensive and comfortable leather chairs in the corner. He turned to the adjacent bar and poured himself three fingers of twenty-year-old Macallen, then settled into one of the chairs. He placed his laptop in his lap and chuckled to himself. *I guess that's how they got the name laptop*, he thought. He opened one encrypted file that contained copies of personal documents and a few pictures of people he once cared about. Maybe part of him still cared. Otherwise, why keep them? Why look at them?

He found the picture he was looking for and enlarged it. It was a picture of the United States Navy Concert Band French Horn section, where he saw a slightly younger version of himself standing next to another horn player with bright red hair.

He held up his drink and said out loud, "Here's to you, Mac." He downed the drink and started to close the file but found himself lingering with it just a little longer than usual. "Damn," was the only other word he could think to say.

# Chapter 3

McKenna jumped out of bed to see that Mac was already on her feet, too. "What is that?" she asked with panic in her voice.

"Fire alarm," Mac calmly replied.

"Then we've got to get out of here!" McKenna exclaimed with a rise in her level of panic. She started for the door, but Mac held out an arm to stop her, shook her head, and put a finger to her lips.

"Stay away from the door," Mac whispered.

McKenna was confused as Mac walked to the window and opened it. There was no balcony, but the windowsill on the outside had a short ironwork frame around it, ostensibly to keep people from jumping out. However, they were only on the second floor, and Mac seemed to think that gave them an exit option other than the door. Still, it was too long a drop to take without risking serious injury.

Mac pulled the top sheet from one of the queen-sized beds, leaned out the window, and tied the sheet to the frame. Then she threw two pillows out the window. "Come on!" she said to McKenna.

"Are you crazy?" McKenna anxiously whispered, looking at her sister, certain the answer was "yes."

Mac grabbed her arm and told her to work her way down the sheet to the windowsill for the room below them and wait for her. McKenna shook her head, and Mac pushed her toward the window.

"Now!" Mac said.

McKenna struggled to climb down on the sheet and lost her grip two feet above the windowsill below. She grabbed at the iron frame and managed to slip one arm around it, but she knew she didn't have enough upper body strength to hold on much longer. Suddenly, Mac was standing on the windowsill and pulled her up.

Mac locked eyes with her. "Kenna, listen to me." McKenna nodded. "We're going to have to get to the ground from here."

"You mean jump?" McKenna shook her head. "We're still too high!"

"No," Mac said. "We can do this, but it's important that you do exactly what I say. Do you understand?"

McKenna reluctantly nodded.

"I'm going to go first," Mac said. "Watch what I do, and then you do the same thing. If you can't, I'll break your fall."

Mac didn't give her time to argue. She climbed over the frame and launched herself from it, managing to grab onto the frame of the windowsill below momentarily before landing on the ground below while simultaneously rolling her body.

McKenna heard a knock on the door.

A male voice said, "There's a fire, and we're evacuating the building! You must leave now!"

"A man is at the door!"

"Get your ass down here now!" Mac ordered.

McKenna was terrified, but the urgency in Mac's voice was clear. She climbed over the frame and dropped by trying to swing herself over enough to land on the windowsill below, but she had overcompensated. She landed on the sill, and her body banged against the window and bounced back against the frame, which loosened with the impact. She was rattled for a moment and shook her head.

"Come on!" Mac ordered again.

McKenna threw one leg over the frame and then the other and worked her hands to the bottom of the frame. She closed her eyes and pulled up the image in her mind of Mac dropping and rolling. She took a deep breath and let go. She managed the drop part but didn't manage the roll part. Fortunately, she dropped with less force than Mac had fallen, and Mac collected the two pillows and used them to break McKenna's fall.

"Are you okay?" she asked. McKenna nodded.

Just then they heard three quick popping sounds coming from what had been their room.

"Let's get out of here," Mac said, grabbing McKenna's arm. "Stay close to the building and follow me."

McKenna followed her sister against the wall for about thirty yards to the right, toward the back of the building until they were in an area devoid of light, then ducked behind the box shrubs that surrounded the building.

"Stay low, "Mac said, lowering herself and creeping around the back edge of the line of shrubs, looking toward the window of their hotel room.

A figure in a black hoodie looked out the window into the night sky that was punctuated by outdoor lights mounted at regular but sparse intervals around the hotel. The hooded person held up a flashlight, looking first to the left, then straight ahead, then to the right. McKenna followed Mac as she ducked lower behind the shrub.

"Come on," Mac whispered as she led them back the way they had come.

"Where are we going?"

Mac's response was a finger to her lips demanding silence. They passed the point where they had landed on the ground and moved toward the back corner of the building. She watched as Mac counted the seconds and then gingerly peeped around the corner. "No one is there," she whispered. "Follow me." When they reached the back door, Mac pulled out her room key card and swiped it to unlock the door. Mac pressed her finger against her lips again, and McKenna nodded.

They slowly moved up the stairs until they reached the second floor. They peered through the small rectangular window in the door to the hall and saw no one, so Mac quietly opened the door. They both slipped into the hallway. Their room—and hopefully George—was on the hall a few doors down. The alarm was still blaring, but no one appeared to be around. She heard sirens and saw a reflection of flashing red lights from the window near the door.

They moved down the hall, and although they listened closely, they heard nothing but sirens. The rooms they passed were quiet. Finally, they reached the corner that led to the hall where their room was. Mac peeped around the corner. "I think something's wrong with George," she whispered. As they rounded the corner, they saw George, sitting in his chair with his head leaning against the window. The lock on the door to their room had been obliterated.

"Do you think those are the shots we heard?"

"Yeah, I do," Mac said quietly. She motioned for McKenna to stay where she was, then she sprinted forward and pulled George's gun from its holster. McKenna stared in disbelief as Mac edged her way back to the door of their room and pushed the door completely open with her foot, keeping her eyes and the weapon on the room as she entered, sweeping the gun back and forth and then pushing open the door to the bathroom and repeating the process. McKenna felt like she was watching a scene from a movie. *When did she learn to do this?* She watched as Mac ran to the window and peeped outside. McKenna slipped in behind her. Fire trucks and police cars lit up the lanes in front of the building. Beyond them was a large group of people in pajamas, robes, and other hurriedly gathered clothing. Then Mac's eyes caught movement on the tree line, and she thought she saw a figure in a hoodie moving away from the hotel.

They returned to the hallway and turned their attention to George, who was suddenly sitting upright in his chair and looking directly at Mac.

"What are you doing with my gun, Ms. Hollingsworth?"

Mac handed the weapon back to George and said, "I asked you to call me Mac, Captain. Are you okay?"

\* \* \*

The once again unsuccessful assassin made his way to the tree line and moved methodically into the cover provided by the trees. *Who the hell are these women?* he thought as his disbelief at their escape gave way to frustration and anger. *I'm not checking in*, he thought, *not right now anyway. I'm going to see if I can locate them and end this thing first.*

From the cover of the trees, he observed the crowd of people who had evacuated the hotel. The lights in front of the hotel and the front parking lot provided adequate light for him to scan the faces in the crowd to see if his target was among them. They weren't.

*They can't have gone far*, he assured himself, *but which direction made the most sense?*

He cautiously worked his way through the trees toward the back of the hotel. The back parking lot contained about a dozen vehicles, one of which was the police car that had delivered the women to the hotel. It was empty. He noticed another car, a black Ford Interceptor, a car he knew was common for law enforcement. No insignia or markings on it, but a man was sitting behind the wheel on his cell phone.

He watched as the man concluded his conversation and put down his phone before exiting the vehicle with his weapon drawn, scanning the parking lot and the trees beyond.

The assassin pulled back farther behind a large oak tree, certain its size was sufficient to conceal him. He waited a few moments before risking a look around the great tree. The man in the car had donned night vision goggles and was repeating his scan of the area. The assassin pulled back quickly to fully conceal himself again. He saw the man with the night vision goggles suddenly turn his head quickly in his direction, as if the man had seen movement. He remained motionless as the man with the goggles continued to look for any other movement. Finally, the man pulled off the night vision goggles, took out his cell phone, and quickly tapped in a contact. The assassin smiled. The man's distraction gave him enough time to roll undetected to a group of hydrangeas that put him not only closer but also parallel to the other armed man.

* * *

"Are we clear down there?" George asked his partner Leo.

"I'm not sure," Leo replied. "I saw movement in the trees a minute ago, but nothing since. I'll cover you if you want to bring them down to the car."

"I don't think so, partner. I'm still not 100% from whatever they hit me with."

"So what's the plan, George?" Leo's frustration came through in his voice. "You can't stay where you are. It's not secure."

"Yeah, yeah, I know," George said, trying to clear his head. He looked at an impatient Mac, who threw up her arms in a 'what's-the-plan' gesture.

"Okay, okay," George responded, as much to Mac as to his partner. "We're coming down." He reached into his ankle holster and pulled his secondary weapon. "But, Leo," he said as he handed Mac the weapon, "I'm arming Ms. Hollingsworth, so just be aware."

"You're what?" Leo said, but George had already disconnected the call.

"I trust you know how to use that?" George nodded at the weapon in Mac's hand. She gave him a look that silently conveyed she not only knew how to use it but also that she was insulted that he asked.

Mac slipped out the magazine, returned it, and put one in the chamber, satisfied that the weapon was loaded and ready. McKenna's eyes were wide as she watched this exchange and opened her mouth to speak, but nothing came out. Mac smiled at her sister and once again put her finger to her lips.

"Just stay behind me," she said.

"Okay," added George, "let's go."

The trio approached the door to the stairs with their backs against the wall. When they reached the door, George looked through the vertical window, seeing nothing and no one but knowing that his field of vision was obscured. He motioned to Mac that he was going to open the door and wanted her to cover him. She nodded.

George opened the door, quickly scanning first left and right then down into the stairwell. He motioned with his head for the sisters to follow him. They slowly worked their way to the ground floor to the back door that Mac and McKenna had used to reenter the hotel. He looked through the door window but didn't see Leo anywhere. He pulled out his cell phone and dialed. No answer. *Shit*, he thought. Then he dialed the dispatcher.

"This is Captain George Gordon. Ping my vehicle and send backup immediately."

"Understood, Captain," the dispatcher replied.

# Chapter 4

The man behind the desk could feel his level of anxiety increase with each passing minute. He'd been waiting hours for confirmation that the assassin had finally been successful but had received no such information. Part of him also felt relieved he hadn't received that call.

His thoughts turned to the strange turn of events that had landed him in this situation. He had worked hard to be accepted into the Navy Band. He completed both a bachelor's degree and master's degree in music with the French Horn as his focus of study. It seemed like the perfect option to get paid for something he loved doing, and his successful tryout for the Navy Concert Band was a way to do that while also serving his country. It might have even made his father proud of him for the first time.

He had been involved with music since he signed up for a class in the fifth grade. He wasn't athletic at all, and he had learned that signing up for band would get him out of physical education class. The band director handed him a trumpet and gave him some rudimentary instructions on how to play. He told the band director he didn't know how to read music, but the director told him not to worry about that. It was part of what he would be learning.

He left school that day with a form for his parents to sign and a trumpet that, although it had obviously seen many years of use, looked bright and shiny to him. It made him feel special—something he had never felt before.

When he got home that day, he noticed his father's rusted pickup truck parked on the grass near the house. He remembered feeling anxious then, too, and remembered thinking, *That can't be good.* And it wasn't.

He gingerly opened the wood screen door and tried to quietly slip inside, but he wasn't used to carrying a trumpet along with his schoolbooks. The screen door bumped against the trumpet case as it closed. His mother emerged from the kitchen and greeted him with one finger on her lips and another pointing at his father, who was asleep in the recliner. The boy nodded.

He and his mother approached the stairs to go to his bedroom where they could talk without waking his father, but the boy's clumsiness with the trumpet case caused him to bump into the stair railing. That, along with the ever-creaking first step, made their successful escape impossible.

"What's all the racket?" his father shouted as he sat up in the recliner, rubbing his eyes. "What's that you got there, boy?"

He remembered the panicked look he gave his mother, who tried to intervene by saying, "It looks like David is going to be in the marching band at school."

"Marching band?" his father said with obvious distaste. "That's for sissies, son."

David felt like his feet were stuck to the floor. His heart was pounding, and he couldn't move. But he surprised himself with a bold move to speak. "I'm not good at sports, Dad, but I will be good at this."

His father rubbed his sleepy eyes as he studied the small boy. "Well," he said, "you'd better be more than good at it then. You'd better be the best."

David worked tirelessly on learning how to play the trumpet and how to read music. He practiced most often when his father was at work. For as long as he could remember, his father had made it clear that he was a disappointment. Although he never abused him physically, the harsh criticism and cruel words took a heavy toll on David's emotional development, compromising his self-esteem.

In music, however, he learned that he had value. His band director was impressed with his rapid progress and quickly added him to the middle school band, two years before he anticipated.

On his first day as part of the band, he noticed a strange-looking horn that was larger than a trumpet and its brass curled around in a curious circle. He had never seen a French Horn and didn't realize that's what he was seeing. As the "new kid" and the least experienced player, he sat in the last seat of the trumpet section. There were four of these strange but beautiful instruments in the row in front of him.

The band director, Mr. Stacy, took the group through their warm-up and tuning exercises before turning to a piece of music the group had been working on for their spring concert. It was a simple orchestration of the opening theme of the movie, *Star Trek: First Contact*, which began with a solo segment by the French Horn section.

As the horns began to play, David's mouth fell open in awe. He had never heard a sound like they made. He didn't understand why, but he became aware that there were tears in his eyes, which he quickly brushed away before anyone else might see them.

After the rehearsal, Mr. Stacy came over to David as he was packing up his trumpet and asked him if he had enjoyed his first rehearsal with the group.

David nodded shyly, then blurted out, "It was great!"

Mr. Stacy patted him on the back and smiled. "Welcome to the band, David. I think you're going to be pretty great, too!"

Mr. Stacy walked back to his desk in the corner of the room and responded to the questions of a few other students before turning to the small pile of music on his desk. He turned to file some of the scores in the filing cabinet behind his desk and seemed surprised when he turned back around and saw David standing there.

"David, I thought you had left already. Is there something you need?"

David's typical shyness seemed to have suddenly disappeared as he looked directly into the director's eyes. "Mr. Stacy, what are those big, curly horns that are in the row in front of the trumpet section?"

"They're French Horns," he responded kindly. "They're pretty, aren't they?"

David nodded, then found the directness of his words blurting out of him again. "I want to play one of those." He paused, searching for some expected negative reaction from the director. "Can I? Please, Mr. Stacy?"

The director sat back in his seat and asked David to pull up a chair. "You want to know if you can change your instrument to the French Horn instead of a trumpet?" David nodded. "Why do you want to change, David?"

David struggled to find the right words. "It's the way they look and the sound they make." He paused a moment before adding, "I don't think I've ever wanted something so bad."

David's heart was pounding, but he remained silent. He had never spoken to a teacher – to anyone – so boldly. Mr. Stacy cocked his head and gave David a curious look. *Is he gonna be mad at me?* But Mr. Stacy wasn't angry with David. He asked him to sit down so they could talk for a few minutes.

"It's a bit harder to play than the trumpet is. Are you sure you want to try something that's harder?"

"Yes. I really want to. Can I?" David was embarrassed that he was almost begging but he couldn't stop himself. He felt almost like he was hungry but hungry in a way he had never felt before.

"Okay, young man," the director said, looking at his watch. "What class are you supposed to be in right now?"

"It's my library time. I usually do some of my homework there.

Mr. Stacy picked up the phone and asked the principal to excuse David from his library time that day because of a special project he was working on with him. The principal approved it and told the director he would notify David's teacher.

"This is my prep period," Mr. Stacy said. "I don't have another class until next period." The director went to the large storage room next to his desk and came back with an oddly shaped instrument case, which he put on the floor next to his desk. He took out a French Horn and its mouthpiece. He sprayed the mouthpiece with a special sanitizer, inserted it into the horn, and handed it to David. "Okay, young man," he said, smiling, "let's see what you can do."

David's trip down memory lane was interrupted by his phone ringing.

"Yeah, it's me. What's up?"

"I just got off the phone with someone I trust. It seems that Ms. Hollingsworth may no longer be in the Navy. She's now somehow connected to the NSA."

David sat down behind his desk, leaned back in his chair, and closed his eyes. "Just when I thought this situation couldn't get any worse."

# Chapter 5

The assassin watched as George eased the door open and scanned the surrounding area with what little light the parking lot provided. When George paused to focus on part of the woods near the hydrangeas, the assassin lay still, fearing he might have been spotted. He began to think of possible escape plans until he saw a deer emerge from the tree line. He smiled as George turned away.

He had seen George but saw no sign of the two women. Then two police cars came around the corner of the hotel with lights and sirens.

*Damn*, he thought, *I've got to get out of here.*

He was angry that Mac and her sister had somehow slipped away, but he knew they hadn't left in the police car or the unmarked Interceptor. Those remained in the parking lot, and the other detective he'd seen was out of commission. The longer he remained in the hydrangeas, the harder the women would be to find and the chance of being seen by the arriving police increased. He crawled slowly back toward the trees, scanning for enough cover to get away from the hotel and all the attention it now had.

When he finally found enough trees to obscure his presence. He glanced back toward the rear door of the hotel. He saw George move between the cars and crouch again to check on his partner, who was breathing, but unconscious—the side of his head grazed with a bullet. Just before he turned to disappear into the trees and began to think of his next steps, he saw his redheaded target come out the door, her hands in the air with a small gun dangling from one finger with her sister behind her.

George stood up and moved in front of Mac and McKenna. He held up his badge to the arriving officers and yelled, "Don't shoot!"

The assassin cursed again as he ran deeper into the trees. He gritted his teeth in anger. What had only been a dispassionate, business-as-usual task now felt more personal. His emotions were a strange mix of admiration for her skill in eluding him and the pure rage that he felt.

Finally, he reached his car, his right leg aching in its prosthesis from the extended run. He sat in the dark and tried to clear his head. Nothing was going right on this case. What would happen if—or when—he reported that he had once again failed his mission? *Why do they want her dead?* he thought, surprising himself. He had never asked that question before. It never seemed to matter. Did it matter now? *Why* did it seem to matter now? He banged his head against the headrest.

"I can't think right now," he said to himself out loud. "I need food and coffee."

\* \* \*

McKenna was silent as they found themselves back in Captain Vick's car once again. She hadn't spoken a word since leaving the hotel. Mac rested her head on the back of the seat. She was tired and needed sleep. She was angry and needed answers. She allowed her thoughts to drift back to when everything in her life seemed to go sideways.

It had been only a couple of months ago. The Navy Band had just finished a month-long tour of performances at U. S. Naval bases in Europe. She was looking forward to a few days of leave before rehearsals and related duties began again at the Navy Yard in D.C.

They had arrived at Joint Base Andrews late on a Tuesday evening. She had left her car at McKenna's house while she was away, and her friend, Sally—the band's Principal Flute player—had offered to drive her home, but Sally's boyfriend, Stewart, suggested they could use the few days' leave to spend some much-needed "alone time" together.

David seemed to be lagging behind the group in gathering his horn and duffle bag and jumped into the conversation. "Hey, Mac," he said as he edged over to their small group. "I can drop you off."

Mac shrugged and smiled at Sally and Stewart. "You two have a great time!" she whispered. "I'll see you Friday." She smiled as her friends walked away together. She and Sally always took turns driving each other home after a tour, but she knew the relationship between Sally and Stewart had grown increasingly serious. She was happy for them to have a couple of days off together. "Thanks, David," she said as she gathered her horn and duffle. "Where's your car?"

She and David were both horn players, but she never really considered him a friend. She always sensed some unspoken discomfort when they were near each other—and they were almost always near each other. She was Principal French Horn, and he was Alternate Principal, so they sat next to each other. She sometimes wondered if he was jealous of her position but dismissed that idea. He had never said anything to indicate he felt that way. They performed well together in the horn section but still...

Their conversation in the car was limited to her giving him directions and an occasional comment about the concert tour and the long trip home. When they arrived at Mac's apartment, however, David came around to the passenger side of the car and pulled Mac's horn and duffle from the back seat. She reached to take them from him.

"No, I've got it. You get the door."

Mac unlocked her door and once again reached for her horn and duffle. "Thanks for the ride, David. I appreciate that." She started inside and noticed he remained standing by the door.

He smiled at her. "No problem, Mac. Any time." Instead of walking away, though, he leaned against the door frame. She looked back at him with raised eyebrows. "I was just thinking that we've never really taken the time to get to know each other. I could use a drink before calling it a night." He looked down and then back up to meet her eyes. "Mind if I come in for a while?"

Mac hoped she was successful in masking her surprise at his behavior, and it took her a few seconds to verbalize a reasonably calm response. "You're right," she agreed, "we've never really talked very much." David shifted as if he was about to come inside, but Mac continued, "But tonight is not a good night. I'm really tired, David. I mean it's like what—one o'clock in the morning?" She smiled and shook her head. "Maybe another time."

David didn't move right away. He seemed to be trying to think of something else to say but finally decided this was not the time. "Sure," he said, smiling again. "Good night, Mac. See you Friday."

"Good night, David," she said, keeping her voice even, "and thanks again for the ride."

She closed her apartment door and locked it, then flipped on the light nearest the door to find her way around the dark apartment. She parked her horn in her practice area in the dining room and took her duffle bag to her bedroom to unpack it before going to bed.

*That was a strange conversation*, she thought. *I wonder what that was all about.* David had never expressed an interest in even friendship with her. *Was that a pass?*

She shook her head and decided it was not something she wanted to think about tonight. She just wanted to sleep. She finished putting her clothes away, dropped a few things in her laundry basket, and slipped on a T-shirt and pajama bottoms. She walked to the kitchen to get a glass of water and turn out the light by the door. She drank her water then returned the glass to the kitchen. As she put the glass in the sink, she casually glanced out the sheer curtain covering the window above the sink. David's car was still outside.

\* \* \*

In the back seat of Captain Vick's cruiser, McKenna glanced over to Mac, whose head rested against the back of the seat, her eyes closed.

*My God, is she asleep? How could she possibly be asleep after everything they had been through?*

The fear and chaos that had taken over her brain in the last few hours seemed to be clearing a little, but only a little. She was suddenly aware that her whole body seemed to be shaking. She closed her eyes and took some deep breaths, focusing on the simple act of breathing and visualizing the air as she inhaled and exhaled and as the air moved throughout her body. It was a process she had learned at a retreat she had attended many years ago and was one of several tools she had learned there to manage the anxiety that had been a part of her life for as long as she could remember.

Gradually, she felt her body begin to relax. Her breathing began to slow down, the shaking became less evident. She told herself she was safe. *Safe? Was she?* The events of the day threatened that idea. She altered her self-talk, telling herself that right now, at this moment—in the back of a police cruiser with two armed officers in the front seat focused on the safety of her and her sister—at this moment, she was safe. She consciously moved the larger question of safety to a "box" in her mind, a box she would open later when she felt ready to process it. She knew she needed to replace those thoughts, though, lest they jump out of the box and back into her mind. That was another thing she had learned at the retreat—the "white bear thing"—that if you try not to think about white bears, you will find white bears take over your thoughts. She had to replace the thoughts with something else to keep those safety questions—her "white bears" of the moment—from tormenting her.

Her "go-to" replacement thought for a long time was to think of the Steppenwolf song, "Magic Carpet Ride." This time, however, as she began to let her mind move through the song, she felt herself laugh. She had used these tools many times over the years but never in a situation as extreme as the one she now found herself in.

*If it works for me in the middle of all this, then I guess all those years of practice really have paid off.*

Her laugh drew the attention of the other three people in the car. The officers in the front seat stopped talking to look back at her, and Mac awakened and looked at her curiously.

Captain Vick spoke the question on everyone's mind, "Are you okay, ma'am?"

McKenna appreciated the concern in his voice, but she also thought it was a stupid question. She chuckled. "Yeah, I'm just fine, Captain. It's been just another day in the life of an IT manager." No one responded to her comment, so she decided it might be a good time to open that box in her mind. "I would, however, like to know what the hell is going on." She turned to Mac. "Can someone in this car please explain that to me?"

For McKenna, the silence in the car seemed to last much longer than it probably did.

Finally, Captain Vick glanced at Mac. "Right now, ma'am, I think your sister is the only one in this car who has that information."

Mac looked at McKenna and then turned to Captain Vick. "Captain, I need to make a secure phone call."

McKenna's mouth fell open. She wasn't sure what she had expected to hear next, but what Mac said wasn't on the list of possibilities. "You need to do *what*?"

If Captain Vick was surprised by Mac's statement, his expression didn't show it. He simply sighed, then nodded. "Okay, Ms. Hollingsworth, I think we can manage that."

"Please call me Mac, Captain. Everyone does."

\* \* \*

The assassin fulfilled his need for food and coffee by driving through a Starbucks in a strip mall nearby. He received his coffee, turkey and Swiss sandwich, and a chocolate croissant and moved to a less crowded section of the parking lot.

*Maybe that shot of espresso will help me figure out what the hell I should do. Why am I wondering about this target—this woman?*

He took a bite of his sandwich, stretched his neck, and then settled against the headrest.

Then it hit him. She reminded him of his fiancé, Jessica, who died in the accident that also resulted in him losing his right leg. The drunken officer who hit them was serving a long prison sentence, but it didn't seem like enough. That guy had cost him everything he cared about—his fiancé, his leg, and his career in the Navy. He could have made different choices. With his service record and security clearance, he could have gotten a job as a contractor or consultant and made a good living for himself, but he was angry and bitter—so angry and bitter that he didn't want to work for anything even remotely related to the government in general and to the military in particular.

The Hollingsworth woman didn't really look like Jessica Jessica had straight, auburn hair, and the Hollingsworth woman had flaming, curly red hair. So it wasn't the hair, it was something else—something he couldn't immediately figure out—something about the way she moved, the way she handled herself, the way she seemed to outsmart him, which was not an easy thing to do. Jessica had been a bit like that. She always seemed to know what he was thinking or what he was going to do or say almost before he knew it. Was that it?

He finished his sandwich, washing it down with his espresso-enhanced coffee. He took the chocolate croissant from the wrapper and noticed it was still warm. Rather than taking a bite, though, he stared at it. *It's warm. I don't have much in my life that's warm anymore.* He looked out the car window at people coming and going—individuals who seemed to move with a purpose, or at least a goal; a few couples on their way to or from some destination where they would be together.

He felt moisture building up in his eyes. *Tears? Really?* Hell no! He shook his head. *Get a grip, man! This is stupid!* He downed the rest of his coffee and threw the warm chocolate croissant out the window before driving out of the parking lot and heading back to his hotel room.

The excitement at the hotel had ended. The fire department had determined that there was no fire, but someone had intentionally set off an alarm. The fire trucks, paramedics, and police cars no longer crowded the parking lot in front of the building. He drove down one side of the building and exited on one of the back streets. He noticed there were still a few police cars at the back of the building. He sighed and slapped the steering wheel.

*Looks like I need to wait a little longer before going back. Just drive*, he told himself.

He drove, but he felt like he was wasting time. He also felt confused about what to do next. He had no home to go to, no friends to hang out with, and he certainly didn't want to check in with David. He thought about Jessica. She wouldn't like the man he had become—taking out his rage by killing people for whoever paid him enough to do it.

*Money*, he thought, *I have more than I would ever need, so what was the point?*

He had no one to share it with. His mind turned back to the horror of the night she was killed, and he suddenly remembered something he had filed away in some dark recess of his mind. They were on their way home from a celebratory dinner that night. They were celebrating because Jessica told him she was pregnant.

His rage and grief converged into a spiral within him, threatening to suck him down to a place of no return. He pulled into a convenience store parking lot, put the car in park, and began to sob.

# Chapter 6

Mac rested her head on the back of the seat again. There was no conversation among any of the occupants in the car. The silence, however, spoke volumes. She knew that everyone in Captain Vick's cruiser wanted information from her—information she was not at liberty to share until she spoke with her case officer at NSA.

She never wanted to be involved in all of this. It had put an end to her naval career and probably also to any hope of a career as a musician. She closed her eyes, and her mind took her back to the day everything started going sideways.

It was the day after David had dropped her off at her apartment. The day after she noticed that he lingered in his car long after they had said goodnight to each other. The next morning, she began her usual routine of unpacking, doing laundry, and clearing the dust out of her apartment after a long time away. She also decided she needed to do some cleaning and maintenance on her horn. It was hard to do it as thoroughly as she liked when the band was traveling, but she was home for a while now. Today seemed like a good time as she waited for the washing machine to finish its cycle.

She took her horn into her bedroom and laid it on her bed. Next to it, she laid a large, thick towel and her small collection of maintenance supplies. She removed all the slides and put them aside before taking the "naked" horn into the bathroom, where she ran warm water through it, and then added a mild cleanser. She methodically turned the horn around slowly several times, allowing the cleanser to move through nearly twenty feet of brass before running water through it again until it ran clear.

She then dried it off, returned to the bedroom, and placed it on the towel. She gathered the slides and took them into the bathroom to complete the same process. After the slides were cleaned and rinsed, she returned them to the towel on the bed as well. She opened an accessory bag and took out a small cleaning snake and began to run it through each of the slides. However, when she came to the smallest slide—the slide for the B flat "trigger" of the double horn—the snake didn't move through. She tried snaking it from both sides of the slide. Something was blocking it.

*Well, that's never happened before*, she thought.

She worked the snake through the slide again and added gentle pressure, trying to dislodge the blockage. After a few minutes of gentle prodding, the blockage emerged at the other end of the slide. *What the hell?* The object lying on the towel was a tiny vial of liquid, and the vial was enclosed in a kind of plastic cover.

Mac stared at the vial for a moment but didn't touch it. She certainly had not put this thing in that slide. Someone else did.

*But who would have—could have—done such a thing and for what purpose?* she wondered.

She picked up her phone and called the office of her commanding officer, Captain Jamison. The captain's aide answered the phone.

"Hi, Jennifer, it's Mac Hollingsworth."

"Oh, hi, Mac! Welcome back!" Jennifer chuckled. "Sorry, I didn't plan for that to rhyme! How are you!"

"Well, I'm not sure. I'd love to catch up with you sometime soon, but right now I need to speak to the captain. Is he in?"

"I didn't expect him to be in today, but he is here. Hang on for a second."

A Sousa march played as Mac waited on hold.

"Hi, Mac," Jamison said. "I figured you were taking advantage of some much-needed R&R. What's up?"

"I'm not sure what's up, sir. I was cleaning my horn and just found something that shouldn't have been there—a vial of some kind of liquid, I think, and the vial is in a plastic cover. What would you like for me to do with it, sir?"

Jamison was caught off guard for a moment. "A vial of liquid, you say?"

"Yes, sir. At least that's what it looks like to me."

"Have you touched it?"

"No, sir, at least not with my hands. I was snaking a slide and realized something was blocking it. I kept gently pushing with the snake, and this thing came out onto a towel on my bed."

"Okay. Don't touch anything now, of course. I'm going to come by your place and take a look. I may have an NCIS agent join me there, just to be on the safe side."

"Yes, sir. I'll see you soon."

Mac ended the call and sat in the chair next to her bed, dumbfounded—but only for a moment. Then she remembered David's strange behavior the night before—first offering her a ride home then acting like he wanted to come in. These were things he'd never done before. Then she remembered the way he lingered in his car long after he should have left. A few days later, he suddenly left the Navy, and no one seemed to know where he'd gone. Did he have something to do with this?

Mac's thoughts returned to the present as she felt a familiar ache in her chest. Her life changed after that day in a way she could never have imagined. Captain Vick's cruiser was pulling into the parking lot of the State Police station.

* * *

David found himself wishing he had never gotten into all of this. Things had gone much further than he had ever imagined. It began simply enough. He started smuggling things that he could easily hide in his horn or under the lining of his instrument case. It started with diamonds and other precious stones. He didn't know where they had come from, and he didn't care. It was about the money he could make. He was disappointed in his experience in the Navy Band. He had initially been excited about the opportunity when he was accepted.

After self-sabotage had resulted in other failed auditions, he went to the Navy Band audition with few expectations. Reducing the pressure on himself enabled him to set aside all the negative chatter in his head that had impaired his performance, and his audition was flawless. The Navy was glad to have him, and he was glad to have the opportunity to make a living doing something he loved.

After his first year, he began to want more. He knew that any possibility of promotion—and therefore higher rank and salary—was not only about one's skill as an instrumentalist. It was about leadership—about taking responsibility for some of the collateral duties—the day-to-day tasks that keep the Navy Band operating smoothly. David wasn't interested in doing any of those things, and he knew his career potential would be limited without them.

Mac Hollingsworth joined the Navy Band a year later. Mac was an amazing horn player—a better horn player than he was—and she was also more interested and involved in helping with collateral duties. Over the years, she seemed to be involved in almost everything at one time or another—working as part of the Navy Band Stage Crew, then as Music Librarian, then in Operations, working on logistical matters necessary for national or international tours.

When Principal Horn, Bill Wilson, retired, David had been in the Navy Band for eleven years and Mac had been there for ten. When auditions were held for Principal Horn, he, Art McArthur, and Mac were the ones who auditioned, and Mac was the one chosen. She was not only chosen for that position, but also later received a well-deserved promotion to Chief Musician.

David's envy prevented him from developing a friendship with her that may have helped him understand what made her better. Mac had tried several times to develop a friendship between them. It made sense. They shared a passion for the same thing, and they were both living out their passion in the service of their country.

Eventually, Mac stopped trying. Their relationship continued to be casual but professional. What she didn't know was that over the years, David had resigned himself to the fact that he was never going to displace her. He was stuck. He sometimes considered leaving the Navy, but he wasn't sure where he would go or what he would do. Maybe he could land a symphony position or even a teaching position, but even if he did, he wasn't sure it was enough anymore. His new goal was making money—a lot of money—enough money that he didn't need to depend on anyone or anything else except himself, and a career in the Navy wasn't going to get him where he wanted to go.

His opportunity came one day when he was sitting in a bar in Tel Aviv, where the band had recently performed. He was commiserating with an attractive bartender about the dire outlook of their respective financial futures. When she left their conversation to serve another customer, a man in an expensive-looking suit sat down in the seat next to him.

"Buy you a drink, friend?" the man asked.

David smiled and shook his head. "Sorry, man, I'm not into guys."

"Neither am I," said the man. "What I'm into is making money. It sounds like that might be something else we have in common." The man raised his eyebrows.

"Yeah, I guess it's something else we have in common," David responded, "but I'm only here for a few days. I'm a member of the U.S. Navy Band, and we'll be leaving soon to resume our tour."

The man nodded and took a sip of his drink. "Navy Band, you say? That could be quite helpful."

David was incredulous. "Look, man, I don't know what you have in mind, but I don't see how I can be helpful to you."

"You can be helpful by helping me 'move things,'" he said, making air quotes, "and by helping both of us make more money than you'll ever make in the Navy."

David eyed the man's expensive suit, his expensive shoes, the Rolex he wore on his wrist, and the two diamond rings he wore. He looked like he knew something about making money, probably lots of money.

The man took David's silence as an opportunity. "Let me buy you a drink and tell you how I think you could help. If you're not interested after that," he shrugged, "no harm done. We go our separate ways." He paused for a moment to let the invitation sink in. "What are you drinking, my friend?"

"Scotch," David said simply.

The man tapped on the top of the bar to get the bartender's attention. When she returned to where they were sitting, he said, "Do you have any twenty-year-old Macallan?"

She nodded. "Sure," she said. "It's in the back, though."

"Be a love and get me and my friend a double, please."

"If you're buying me a double Macallan, I probably need to know your name," David said with a smile.

"My name is Eli." He held out his hand to shake David's hand. "That's all you need to know right now."

David shook Eli's hand, but as David listened to Eli, a variety of conflicting thoughts ran through his mind. *It's illegal. It's a lot of money. I could go to prison. No one really gets hurt.*

Finally, Eli finished talking and gave David a chance to ask questions or respond.

"No drugs. No spy stuff. Nothing that can hurt anyone. Right?"

Eli nodded. "No drugs and no spy stuff. Just precious stones. And the only 'hurt' is that the governments involved don't get the tax and tariff revenue they would with traditional trade."

"If I get caught, I'll go to prison," David said more to himself than to Eli.

"There's some risk, yes, but the rewards far outweigh the risks, my friend." Eli took another sip of his Scotch. "I think you have some advantages over the usual smuggler."

David laughed. "Really? What advantages?"

Eli swirled the Scotch in his glass. "Well, you're in the U. S. Navy Band. I suspect when your instruments and equipment are loaded on a plane, they aren't searched."

"Not true," David said. "They run everything through an X-ray like any airport does, then they have dogs trained to sniff out drugs or explosives."

"Drugs and explosives, but not diamonds," Eli responded with confidence, "and X-rays are not a problem. Genuine diamonds are translucent on X-rays. You line the inside of your horn with them, and you should be fine."

David took a sip of his drink. "I don't know." He shook his head. "I've never done anything like that before."

Eli nodded. "Okay, I get that. There's a first time for everything." He paused a moment. "What if I start you out with a small amount so you can try it?"

"What's 'a small amount,' and what would my payout be?"

"Depends on the quality and cut of the stones, but I only move the best." Eli eyed David carefully. "Tell you what," he said. "Let's start you out with just say twenty one-carat stones—conservatively worth," he waved his hand back and forth, "at least $250 to $300 thousand dollars." He paused as David looked up from his drink directly into Eli's eyes. "And I'll sweeten the deal by giving you a bonus on your first run."

"What kind of bonus?" David asked.

Eli nodded. "Normally, your cut would be fifteen percent or about $45,000. For your first run, I'll up that to $60,000."

David spilled a few drops of his Scotch and let out a big sigh. "Look, man, this is a lot to take in. Can I think about it overnight?"

Eli shook his head. "Sorry, my friend, I need an answer now. I don't want to find myself suddenly accosted by customs officials or local police."

Neither of them spoke for several minutes. Finally, David took a long sip of his drink, emptying the glass. "Okay," he finally said. "I'm willing to try one run and see how it goes."

"Excellent!" Eli said as he smiled and placed his hand on David's shoulder. "Let's get down to business!"

\* \* \*

David shook his head and leaned back in his chair. *It was never supposed to go this way*, he thought.

His association with Eli had been very profitable. David had amassed several million dollars over the four years he smuggled for Eli. Then things changed. Eli seemed to have suddenly disappeared, but David was contacted by a woman who said she was a friend of Eli's. They met in a Starbucks in Washington, DC, several blocks from the Navy Yard. The smuggling she wanted him to do had nothing to do with diamonds. She wanted him to smuggle documents but refused to tell him what they were.

"I don't do spy stuff," David told her. "I've been clear about that with Eli from the very beginning."

"It's not 'spy stuff,'" she said. "Well, I guess you could say it's corporate espionage—nothing government-related." She paused to let that sink in. "I will make it worth it to you. I can pay you $50,000 to smuggle a few documents that you can mix in with your music, a book, or in your horn. I don't care how you do it. You just need to pass them along to a contact in Seoul. I believe the Navy Band will be performing in South Korea during your Pacific performance tour next month, yes?"

David took a deep breath. "$50,000 for a few documents? What are they about?"

The woman shook her head. "Trade secrets, I'm afraid. So are you in or not?"

"I'm in," he said as he finished his latte.

Looking back, David realized where things had started to go sideways. He hadn't cared about corporate espionage. It didn't matter to him which company could build a better mousetrap, sensor, or medical device. He cared that he made a lot of money. Eli had instructed him in the finer points of opening offshore accounts so his quick and significant increase in income didn't raise any red flags.

As he gradually saw the numbers in his bank accounts increase, his frustration with the Navy in general, and the Navy Band in particular, also increased. The direct deposit that went into his U. S. bank account each month was a fraction of what he was getting paid for smuggling. He found himself almost insulted by it. The daily duties of his role in the Navy began to seem like a waste of his time. He stopped practicing regularly. What difference did it make? He knew he was never going to rise to Principal as long as Mac was around, and he suddenly realized that it didn't matter to him anymore. He had more important things to think about now. He began to wonder if it was time to resign. He decided that at least one more big payday would help him make up his mind.

The chance for another big payday happened unexpectedly. It was also coincidental with another unexpected event.

One day, during a break in rehearsal, his commanding officer, Captain Jamison, had called him into his office. The meeting was a short one, and it reminded him of something he had read in high school in *The Art of French Horn Playing*, a book by the renowned horn player, Philip Farkas. He didn't remember the exact wording, but he remembered the point the author had made.

*If I miss a day of practice, I notice it. If I miss a couple of days, my fellow musicians notice it. If I miss a week, everyone notices it.*

Jamison had noticed it. And Jamison noticed that other members of the horn section had noticed it. Jamison assured him that no one had said anything, but Jamison was concerned David might be having some kind of personal problem. David had denied that, saying he knew he had made some obvious mistakes lately, but he would make sure it wouldn't happen again.

Jamison was still concerned, but he was also pragmatic. "I hope so, David," he said. "We're a professional organization of musicians that represent not only the Navy but also the United States as a whole. I take that representation very seriously." Jamison paused a moment, leaning back in his chair. "Dismissed."

David stood and said, "Thank you, sir." He left Jamison's office knowing his decision was made and he only needed one last big payday before he resigned.

The opportunity that came his way, however, was not what he expected or hoped for. It came when he met with one of his DC contacts at a Starbucks near Dupont Circle. As they sipped their lattes and made casual conversation, his contact slid a napkin across the table. David waited until his contact's hand moved away from the napkin and small talk resumed before casually resting his left hand on the table near the napkin and, eventually, sliding it into his pocket. It was something small, something hard, a small tube of some kind, maybe?

David waited until the Starbucks crowd thinned out before asking, "Okay, what is it, and what's the plan?"

His coffee companion, whose name he had never known, smiled and said, "It's priceless, but your cut is half a million. That's all you need to know."

David was startled—and confused. He had never been given something so small to smuggle, and he had never been paid so much. "I'm not so sure about that," he said. "What the hell is it?"

The contact took a sip of his coffee, and his expression grew serious. "I can't tell you that, at least not exactly, anyway." He looked around the sparsely populated coffee shop. "What I can tell you is that it made its way to me from Fort Detrick. Do you know what they do there?"

David frowned, then nodded.

"Then that's all you need to know," his contact said. "You need to get this to your contact in Seoul. You get half the payment now and the other half when I verify it's been delivered."

David nodded, then stood to leave, noticing there was a tightness in his chest. A wave of nausea crept over him.

"Oh, there's one more thing you need to know," his contact said. "Don't take the plastic casing off and don't let the tube break." He raised his eyebrows in an unspoken question to see if David understood.

David nodded again, then left his contact at the table. He started to throw away his cardboard coffee cup but then decided to hold onto it. He would need it when he got outside and needed to vomit.

# Chapter 7

Mac, McKenna, and Captain Vick approached a medium-sized concrete structure that looked like a small warehouse or storage container. There were no windows and no signs that identified it as a building affiliated with the Maryland State Police.

"This isn't where we were before," Mac noted as she looked over the face of the structure. McKenna seemed confused.

"No, it's not," Captain Vick replied as he approached a steel door with a keypad on the side. He punched in a code, and the keypad disappeared, revealing a biometric pad on which he placed his hand. An almost imperceptible click sounded, and he opened the door for them to enter first.

Mac hesitated for a moment, looking back at the Crown Victoria they had just arrived in, then looked back at Vick—his uniform, his badge, then meeting his eyes.

"You said you needed to make a secure phone call." He shrugged. "This is the most secure place I know of."

They entered a lobby area just inside the door. There were four waiting-room-type chairs, two on each side of the room. Doors with no windows stood on both sides and to the back of the lobby area. Vick walked to the door straight back and repeated the keypad ritual.

They entered an area with four cubicles in the center, surrounded by offices along the sides. Only two of the cubicles appeared to be staffed. The offices all had windows but were covered with blinds.

They followed Vick to the back of the room to an office that also had biometric access. After completing the access process, Vick once again opened the door for McKenna and Mac to enter before him. It looked like a conference room. There was a large oblong table with chairs along one side that faced a wall with a bank of computer screens.

They followed him to the far corner of the room where he took a seat behind a desk and motioned for them to sit in the two chairs on the other side.

"I know who you are, Mac," he said. "We work for the same agency."

Mac was incredulous. "I don't understand."

Vick nodded, then pulled out his credential wallet and held it up for her to see. "NSA." He handed her the phone lying on his desk. "This line—this room, this building, in fact," he said as he made a sweeping motion with his hand, "is secure. You can make your call, but I'm not sure you will find it necessary."

Mac pulled her cell phone from her pocket. "Oh, it's very necessary," she said, rising from the chair and walking to the back of the room. She made her phone call and then returned to the chair in front of the desk. She held out her hand to shake his hand. "Thank you, Captain. It's a pleasure to meet you." She turned to McKenna. "I don't exactly work for NSA," she said. "I just happen to be involved in something of interest to them."

"I don't understand," McKenna began.

Mac shook her head. "I'm sorry, but I'm very limited in what I can tell you, Kenna. It may sound like a cliché from a spy movie, but it's a matter of national security."

Then McKenna shook *her* head. "You were in the Navy Band. I've seen you perform with them probably a dozen times over the years—Principal Horn. I know how proud you were of that."

Mac nodded. "You're right—and, yes, I was very proud of that." She glanced at Vick for a moment then said, "And I had to give it up because I found myself in a situation I never could have anticipated." Her eyes met McKenna's. "I'm sorry, sis, but I can't go into any more detail than that—at least not at this time."

McKenna was indignant. "Well, that sucks, Mac!" She stood up and began to pace in front of the desk. "We could have been killed at that hotel! We still might be!" She shot an accusing look at Vick.

"No," Mac said in the most consoling voice she could muster. "You don't have to deal with this anymore. They're putting you in protective custody."

"What?" McKenna stopped pacing. "Mac, I have a life. I have a home. I have a job!"

"It's okay, Ms. Hollingsworth," Vick broke in. "Everything will be taken care of."

Vick and Mac shared a look at each other as McKenna plopped herself back into the chair and started to cry.

* * *

The assassin returned to the hotel. No police cars or other emergency vehicles remained in the front or back parking lots. The night shift desk clerk seemed to be preoccupied with his cell phone. The assassin had changed clothes before returning, tossing his pants, shoes, and Ravens sweatshirt into a shopping bag. He now wore blue jeans and a long-sleeved gray T-shirt with a Led Zepplin logo on the front and the list of songs they performed at their 1995 induction into the Rock n' Roll Hall of Fame. The night manager looked up as he walked in and glanced at the T-shirt. He seemed unimpressed.

"Quiet night, huh?" the assassin said with a friendly smile.

"Well, it is now," replied the desk clerk, "but it was wild here a couple of hours ago."

"Yeah, what happened?"

"Aw, some dumbass pulled a fire alarm," the desk clerk said with disdain, then added, "But don't worry, there wasn't any fire."

"Well, that's good to know!" the assassin replied as continued toward the elevator. As soon as the elevator doors closed, he pushed the button for his floor, and his friendly smile faded.

*What the hell am I going to do? I'm not sure I want to do this anymore.*

He leaned against the back of the elevator. This was not a business that was easy to leave. He had people to answer to—people who had paid him a lot of money, including a down payment on this current contract.

He thought about Jessica again and how she would judge his current career. He was still puzzled about this line of thinking. These were things he had never allowed himself to think about before. Why now?

The elevator chimed to announce the arrival at his floor. He tossed the shopping bag on the dresser and fell back on the bed. He closed his eyes and saw Jessica's face, smiling and happy on their last evening out together. There was a goodness about her that captivated him. He had seen so much horror overseas, the violence that people were capable of—violence he learned he was capable of. Jessica possessed none of that. She was loving, kind, and honest to a fault. He often wondered how someone like her could love a guy like him, but she did. He wondered if she would love him now, the man who had become so deeply involved in criminal activity. Then suddenly, it hit him.

That was the difference between this contract and every other contract he had taken. He killed for money, but the people he killed were also criminals of one variety or another. Mac Hollingsworth wasn't a criminal. He didn't know a lot about her, but he knew that. He had researched her as he did all his targets, and there was nothing to suggest criminal activity of any kind. He couldn't figure out why anyone would want her dead. Just like he couldn't imagine anyone wanting Jessica dead—and yet, someone had killed her, using a car as a weapon.

He opened his eyes and stared at the ceiling. His thoughts took him by surprise, but they continued to play out in his head and seemed to get more fully formed and stronger as the minutes passed. A wave of calm came over him, which only confirmed what he wanted—something that only a short while ago had been a passing thought he had dismissed. He took one of his cell phones from his pocket and called his personal service representative at his bank in Grand Cayman. It was late at night in the Caribbean, too, but he knew she would answer. She always did.

"Hi, Tori," he began. "I'm sorry to call so late, but I need a favor."

"Daniel, hello!" she said. He could almost see her smiling through the phone. "What can I do for you?"

"I recently received a wire transfer for $50,000. It was the down payment on a piece of property I was planning to sell, but I've changed my mind." Tori knew there was no property involved, and she asked no questions. "I've already told the potential buyer of my decision. I'd like you to reverse that transaction. Can you do that?" he asked, already knowing she could. She had worked money and computer magic for him many times. He paid her to do so regularly.

"Of course," she said. "I'll take care of it right away." She paused a moment then asked, "Will we be seeing you down here again soon?"

"Perhaps. Thanks, Tori."

"You're welcome, Daniel. Have a good evening."

* * *

Less than fifty miles away, David's phone rang. He recognized the number and answered immediately.

"We have a problem," she said.

"What now?" David sighed.

"Our guy returned the money. What the hell is going on, David?"

David sat up suddenly. "What do you mean he returned the money?"

"I mean exactly what I said. He somehow got the wire transfer reversed," the woman said, annoyed with having to explain the obvious.

David sighed. "Maybe we just need to move on. She was a loose end, but the truth is, whatever damage she may have done is probably already done."

"We don't like loose ends," the woman replied.

"I think we're going to have to live with this one. I learned she's somehow involved with the NSA. I don't think your concern about a loose end that's already unraveled is worth bringing more attention from them than we already have."

The woman was silent for only fifteen seconds, but for David, it felt like an hour. He knew his contact had few, if any, concerns about contract killing, but he also knew she had no desire to throw more money at this particular problem. She had other priorities to consider.

"Maybe another time, then," the woman finally said.

"Perhaps," David said, secretly relieved Mac was no longer a target—at least for now.

"If she's involved with NSA," the woman added, "we have to assume they have the vial. Where are the other two?"

"They're safe for now."

"Where are they?" she insisted.

"Look, I think it's better if you don't know the answer to that right now. I'm the only one who knows—and I'll take care of them."

"I don't like that answer, David."

"Well, that's the answer you've got," he responded, ending the call.

*Well, that was a risky move*, he thought.

He wasn't sure *how* risky it was, but he knew the stakes in this horrific plan were high. What if they came after him now? Would they torture him to get their hands on the other two vials? He took at least some small comfort in the fact that they didn't know exactly where he was. He also knew they were good at finding people who were hard to find, especially when those people had something they wanted.

He thought about his relief about Mac no longer being at risk—if that was true. His reaction surprised him. He sat with that for a few minutes. He had been jealous of her in the Navy Band, but that was hardly worth killing for. The truth was, she hadn't done anything wrong.

*Does she ever do anything wrong?*

He had screwed up by planting the vial in her horn. He knew that. He also knew he had put her life in jeopardy by doing so—not only by the fact that his employer considered her an unacceptable loose end, but also by the fact that if she had accidentally broken the vial, it would have killed her. He had to assume the vial was now in the hands of the NSA. He surprised himself by taking some comfort in that.

It was one thing to smuggle diamonds and industrial secrets. He never considered he was really hurting anyone by doing those things, and he had made a lot of money. But smuggling a biological weapon crossed the line for him, and he had been trying to figure a way out of the situation ever since the vials were given to him.

*Why me? There are spies for that kind of thing. Is that what he had become? What made anyone think that I would be part of a plan to commit mass murder?*

He shook his head. He had no answer to that question, but it did make him wonder. He had never killed anyone and was never party to the killing of anyone—at least not that he knew of until Mac's car exploded. His side business—which had replaced his previous profession—was about money, not killing. But then, he also realized he had never asked questions about the journey the diamonds or the documents had made before making it to him. Maybe people had died in the process. He didn't want to believe that, but it was too late now to think about it. What he needed to think about was what he was going to do to get rid of the other two vials in some way that no one got killed—including him.

David looked around the room in the virtual fortress he had created for himself. Was he safe enough—and even if the answer was yes, would he be able to remain safe enough to get rid of the vials and stay alive when his contact figured out he wasn't going to follow through with the instructions he was given about their delivery? He had made that decision as the wave of nausea came over him the day he was given the vials in Seoul. He wanted no part in terrorism—but he especially wanted no part in terrorism within his own country.

There were, unfortunately, a handful of people who did know where he was.

*What the hell am I going to do about that?*

# Chapter 8

Mac turned to Captain Vick and said, "I need a few minutes alone with my sister."

Vick glanced at McKenna, who had stopped crying and sat silently in her chair. Within the perimeter of swelling, her eyes looked red and far away. "Of course," he said, getting up and walking toward the door. "Just press the call button on my desk phone when you're finished."

Mac looked at her sister. "I'm not sure what to say, Kenna. I never wanted any of this to happen. I never wanted any part of this whole thing."

McKenna cocked her head. "And what exactly *is* 'this whole thing?' I thought you were a horn player in the Navy Band. When did that change? How did you get involved in... whatever this is?"

Mac took a deep breath, then sighed. "I was a horn player in the Navy Band. I worked hard to get there. It was my life, and I loved it. I didn't want to leave." She stood up and paced for a few moments in silence before she sat on the edge of Vick's desk, facing her sister. "I can't tell you everything you want to know. I wish I could. I wish this would all go away."

"So what *can* you tell me, Mac? And what am I supposed to do about *my* life now that I'm part of whatever this is?"

"Someone—a colleague—hid something in my horn, Kenna—something bad. I found it by accident and reported it to my command. Things changed after that. NCIS and NSA got involved in the investigation, and I suddenly found myself separated from the Navy."

"So then you went to work for NSA, right?"

"No, not exactly. Technically, I'm sort of a consultant. They want me to work with them, but..."

"But what?"

"It's just not what I do. It's not something I have *ever* wanted to do. I was proud to serve in the Navy, and you know how much I love playing the horn. This mess has cost me the life I knew and loved."

McKenna looked puzzled. "Why do they want you to work with them so much?"

Mac closed her eyes and sighed again. "They told me it was part of my 'family legacy.'"

"What?" McKenna was indignant. "What the hell does that mean?!"

"The people behind this have been involved for a long time—a very long time." She looked deep into her sister's eyes. "Our parents died trying to take them down."

McKenna frowned. "Our parents died in a plane crash."

Mac nodded. "Yes, they did. We just weren't given the whole story." Mac moved to the chair next to McKenna and turned to face her sister. "Our parents worked for NSA. They had collected key evidence that identified a network of smugglers who had shifted from smuggling drugs, diamonds, and other stuff to smuggling information and other 'things' that threatened national security. The evidence they had collected was with them on a plane on its way back to the US from Seoul. The plane crashed in the Sea of Japan. No wreckage was ever found, and our parents, along with a few other people, were eventually presumed dead. All the evidence they had collected went down with them."

"Our parents were spies?" McKenna asked, her confusion visible in the frown on her face.

"No," Mac said. "They weren't spies. They were analysts, but they sent them into the field because of the relationships they had developed with key resources in Korea. Unfortunately, I can't tell you any more than that—at least not right now."

"So what are we supposed to do now, Mac? What am I supposed to do? When will this all be over?"

"I don't know when it will be over. I wish I did, Kenna." She reached for her sister's hand. "I'm not entirely sure what I'm supposed to do, but I *am* sure that you are supposed to stay safe. NSA will make sure you don't lose everything you've worked so hard for, though, even if that means they find—or create—something else for you, like they did me."

"But that's not the life you want and have worked so hard for, Mac. That's not okay."

"No, it's not. I'm a musician, but I am also a member of the U.S. Navy. Right now, both the Navy and the NSA need me to serve our country in a different way." Mac ran her hand through her hair and looked her sister in the eyes. "The oath I took wasn't about music. It was about defending the Constitution."

"But you're not in the Navy anymore."

"I'm not sure that's entirely true, but I can't go into the details right now. Maybe someday, maybe when all of this is over, but not now."

McKenna looked away. Mac gently touched her sister's shoulder.

"Hey," she said tentatively. "Are we okay? You and me?"

McKenna reached for Mac's hand. "You and me?" she said. "Of course, we're okay, Mac. We've always been okay. This mess we're in is not your fault. I know that."

Mac squeezed her sister's hand and then pressed the call button on Vick's phone as instructed. Vick came back into the conference room and looked first at McKenna, then at Mac.

"Everything okay?"

They both nodded.

"Okay," he said, "then let's roll."

* * *

*So here we are again*, McKenna thought, *back in Captain Vick's car, going God knows where this time.*

Her mind was reeling over the events of the past couple of days. First, Annie, her best friend, was killed after borrowing Mac's car. Then she learned the 'accident' was not an accident at all but a targeted attack, with Mac as the intended victim. If all that wasn't enough, she had learned her parents had worked for NSA and were killed in the line of duty. Now her sister, whom she thought she knew pretty well, was not just a French Horn player in the Navy Band but was also somehow involved with NSA. Then to top it all off, they were placing her in protective custody, her employer being told—*what*? What story would make sense of her sudden disappearance from her job and her life? What story would make this all magically okay? She couldn't imagine. It felt like everything she knew, everything she loved was being snatched away.

*Get a grip, McKenna,* she thought.

Her hands were shaking. No, that wasn't accurate. Everything felt like it was shaking. Anxiety, what a horrible feeling—a feeling that seems to take over one's body and mind. Her eyes were looking out the window of the car, but all she saw was a blur of shapes and lights that only seemed to heighten the terror within, so she closed her eyes against the additional stimulation. She thought of Annie and felt a tear fall down her cheek. They had shared so much together. As her mind ran through the memories and experiences they shared, she found herself at a women's retreat they had attended together many years ago. It was one of the last "adventures"—as they liked to call them—they had together.

One of the workshops during the retreat was about mindfulness meditation and how it could be helpful in so many ways. She found herself falling into an exercise the workshop leader had talked them through. She focused on her breath—only on her breath—coming in and moving out, coming in and filling her body with oxygen and light and calm. Gradually, she felt her breathing slow down and her body begin to relax. What an amazing thing that was at the moment. She felt grateful for that. She felt grateful for many things, not the least of which was being alive after being stalked by a killer.

*No*, she thought, *that's not a good place for your thoughts to go right now. Focus on something else.*

It was hard to do, but she returned to focusing on her breath, this time imagining the oxygen as a golden light circulating throughout her body. It fascinated her. Again, her body relaxed.

*Just stay here a while*, she told herself. *Right here, right now, you're okay.*

Suddenly, she heard the opening guitar riff of "Magic Carpet Ride" running through her mind, and, as before, she laughed.

"Hey," Mac said, as she reached over and took McKenna's hand in hers. "How are you doing?"

"I'm okay, Mac," McKenna said. "I'm okay. I'm grateful to be alive. I'm grateful you're alive. I'm grateful that—at least at the moment—we're both safe."

Mac looked at her sister with renewed interest. "How did you manage to calm yourself down so well—and so quickly?"

McKenna smiled. "It's magic."

"I believe you!" Mac laughed. "Maybe someday you'll tell me about it."

The car stopped, and so did their conversation. The drive was much shorter than either of them expected. They were in the driveway of a modest ranch house on a quiet cul-de-sac. Mac noticed Vick had acquired earbuds since they had left his cement block office.

"We're clear," he said to his partner and driver. "Let's go."

Vick, Mac, and McKenna entered through the garage as the garage door opened seemingly on its own. The other agent remained outside, and as they moved past him, Mac noticed he was joined by a woman who had emerged from the backyard.

The three entered the house through the kitchen door and were greeted by another woman dressed in navy blue sweats and sneakers. Mac judged her to be in her thirties. She had short, light brown hair and seemed to have a solid, medium build. She looked like she belonged in the house, like she was part of this quiet suburban neighborhood—except for the Sig Sauer in the cross-body holster that topped her sweats.

Vick motioned toward her to begin the introductions. "Agent Tosh, this is McKenna and Mac Hollingsworth. McKenna, Mac, this is Nadia Tosh. She's your new best friend. You three get acquainted. I need to step outside and check in with headquarters."

# Chapter 9

David looked around his office; he had worked hard to create this place for himself. It had always been a safe place for him. He wasn't sure that was true anymore. He felt safe enough from those who would send him to prison for smuggling, but after his conversation with the woman on the phone, he no longer felt safe from the powerful people who paid him well to take risks for them. He was certain they would find him if he didn't follow through with their instructions—and he had no intention of following through with their instructions. His phone ended his morbid train of thought. He recognized the number. It was the woman he had just spoken with.

*What now?* he thought. He reached for his phone but stopped short of answering the call. *Which would be worse: answering it or not answering it?* He decided that if he answered it, he might be able to buy himself a little more time. He was wrong.

"What took you so long to answer?" she asked, her irritation obvious.

"I was just..."

"Never mind," she said, "It doesn't matter. Agma wants to speak with you personally. Expect his call in the next few minutes. I suggest you answer it immediately."

David frowned. "Who the hell is Agma?" But she had already ended the call.

*Agma,* he thought, *I haven't heard that name before.*

He reached for the laptop on his desk and opened Google. He didn't expect to find a definitive answer on the Internet, but he thought it might give him some ideas. He typed Agma into the search engine, but none of the results made sense—American Guild of Musical Artists, American Gear Manufacturers Association, a free MMO game—

*Shit*, he thought, *this is not getting me anywhere.*

He knew the vials were from Korea, so he went back up to the search box and typed Agma Seoul. The first few results meant nothing to him, then he saw the fourth result and froze.

*Agma is a Sino-Korean word meaning 'evil' or 'demon.'*

He was still staring at the laptop screen when his phone rang again.

"Oh, shit," he said out loud, louder than he intended to. His mind raced through several options. Should he answer it and get through the call as best he could, or should he grab his go-bag and laptop and disappear? Could he ever disappear well enough that they wouldn't find him?

He swiped the answer feature on his smartphone but didn't speak. The caller waited a few seconds for a response. Then David heard a computer-generated voice.

"Mr. Lindsey, I presume?"

David swallowed. "Yes, sir."

"How do you know that I'm a 'sir?'" the voice answered with a chuckle.

"I..." David struggled to come up with an answer but was interrupted.

"No matter," the voice responded. "I think you know who I am, though, correct?"

"Agma," David managed.

"Yes. I am called Agma. Mr. Lindsey, it seems we have a problem with you completing your delivery. Why is that?"

David's brain scrambled to come up with an acceptable response. "No," he finally said. "No problem. I just need a little more time to retrieve the package."

"Explain."

"I put the vials somewhere safe, and I just need a little time to get to them."

There was silence on the other end of the conversation that lasted only ten seconds but seemed like ten minutes to David.

"I see. How much time do you require?"

"I need three days." David broke out in a cold sweat.

"I will give you two."

"I don't think I can..."

"Oh, but you must, Mr. Lindsey. This is non-negotiable. Do I make myself clear?"

"Yes, but..."

"No. No buts. You will deliver the package within forty-eight hours, or there will be severe consequences." The voice paused for a moment. "Must I tell you what those consequences will be, Mr. Lindsey?"

"No. No, sir."

"Ah, good. Then we understand each other. Excellent." The voice ended the call.

David sat back in his chair and wiped the sweat from his face with his sleeve.

*What the hell am I going to do now? I never intended to get involved with anything like this. I should have turned down this job when it was presented to me. But maybe there would have been 'consequences' for my refusal even then. I think this guy goes by a name that means 'demon' for a reason. I don't want to die over this, and I don't want anyone else to die because of it either.*

He suddenly knew what he had to do. He removed the SIM card from his phone and smashed it with a paperweight on his desk. He grabbed his go-bag and his laptop and took one last look around this virtual fortress he had built for himself—a fortress that was no longer safe—and walked out the door.

\* \* \*

Less than thirty miles away, Mac, McKenna, Nadia, and Vick gathered around the large oak dining room table over a dinner of spaghetti with meat sauce and garlic bread prepared by McKenna and Nadia, accompanied by small talk—until Mac couldn't stand it anymore.

"So what's next?" she pressed, then took the last bite of her garlic bread.

Vick and Nadia shared a look Mac couldn't read.

Finally, Vick said, "What's next is that you and McKenna will remain here with Nadia and a couple of other agents while I go back to NSA for a briefing and see where things stand.

Then Mac and McKenna shared a look.

"For how long?" McKenna finally asked.

Vick started to give them an answer but was interrupted by his phone. He held up his hand in a 'give me a minute to take this' kind of motion, then stepped into the kitchen for privacy.

The three women sat together quietly in a futile effort to hear at least his part of the conversation, but all they heard was him answer the call with "Vick" and then silence for a few minutes before hearing him say, "Understood" and end the call.

He returned to the dining table, put his phone back in his pocket, then folded his hands on the table. "I'm afraid there's been a new development."

All three women turned their attention to him.

"Our plans have changed. Mac, you will be coming with me to NSA, and McKenna, you will remain here."

"I hope you plan to tell us more than that," Mac said, rubbing her temple.

"I'm authorized to tell you part of it," he began. He took a deep breath. "Mac, you probably realize that NSA has been monitoring your phones."

"Well, I didn't know for sure, but I suspected it."

"There was a call to the landline at your apartment. The caller left a voice mail." He looked into Mac's eyes. "Mac, the caller was David Lindsey. He wants to talk with you."

# Chapter 10

Tori Stone, the failed assassin's "special" bank service representative, completed his request to reverse the $50,000 payment he had received. Thirty minutes later, her phone rang again. She thought Daniel was calling her back—that he had either forgotten something or wanted to verify the reversal had been successful, but the new call was not coming from Daniel. She recognized the number, however, and answered immediately.

"Tori Stone."

"Hold for Agma," a female voice instructed.

Tori took a deep breath. She had been on Agma's payroll for the past year but had never spoken with him directly.

"Ms. Stone," the strange, electronic voice began.

"Yes, sir?"

"I understand our mutual acquaintance had you reverse a payment he recently received from us."

"Yes, sir. That's correct."

"An interesting but unfortunate development—at least for him." Agma's electronic voice paused momentarily. "I require your assistance, Ms. Stone."

"Of course, sir. What can I do for you?"

"I want his account to be liquidated. I want it transferred to the account I'm about to give you."

"Of course, sir. I can do that. However, sir..."

"However?" he replied. "Is there a problem, Ms. Stone?"

"No, sir. I thought it was important for you to know that he has two other accounts under two different names at two other banks."

"I see," he said. "That's very helpful information, Ms. Stone. Do you have access to these other accounts?"

Tori hesitated.

"Ms. Stone?" he prompted.

"It won't be easy, sir, but I believe I can access them."

"Very good. I want you to transfer the balance of those other accounts as well. You may, however, transfer ten percent into your own accounts as a bonus for services rendered."

"That's very generous, sir. Thank you—but, sir, he is going to know I'm the one who has done this. He may come after me."

"He will not, Ms. Stone. Before he has had a chance to know what has happened, he will no longer need these accounts. He will not be a problem for you. Do I make myself clear?"

"Yes, sir." Tori suddenly felt light-headed and momentarily found it difficult to breathe. She was about to become a very wealthy woman, but that wealth meant betraying a client who had trusted her for several years longer than she had worked for Agma.

"Are you prepared to take the account information for these transfers?"

"Yes, sir."

Tori wrote down the account information and then repeated it back to him for verification. He acknowledged that the information was correct, and then he ended the call.

* * *

Immediately after his conversation with Tori, Daniel had booked a private plane under one of his aliases. He couldn't stay in DC, and, despite his suggestion to Tori that she might see him soon, he didn't feel safe going to Grand Cayman after reversing his recent payment. He needed a safe place to consider where he might go to escape the inevitable wrath of his employer. He decided to fly to a resort in Bermuda where he owned a cottage under yet another alias. From there, he could think through a plan to disappear.

As he boarded the plane, he told the pilot to take him to Grand Cayman, but once they were in the air, he told him to change course and take him to Bermuda. He had flown with this pilot many times and had never had any reason to distrust him—except Daniel mistrusted everyone, especially after he bailed on his last assignment. He slept on the five-hour flight to L.F. Wade International Airport on St. George's Island. The cottage was a convenient ten-minute drive in his electric car that awaited him at the airport.

Once he arrived at his cottage, he carefully checked the surrounding area for suspicious activity and found none, so he entered his cottage and just as carefully cleared each room for safety and security. The cottage appeared secure but smelled musty. He hadn't been there in several months, and because of the nature of this sudden trip, he hadn't called housekeeping to prepare the cottage in the usual way. He didn't mind musty right now. It was more important to limit the number of people who knew he was there. He secured the cottage by making sure the doors and windows were locked and setting his security system. Only then did he feel confident enough about his safety to prepare for the tasks at hand.

It was noon when he wrapped his laptop in a beach towel, donned swim trunks, and walked down to the private beach, stopping at a deli on his way to pick up a sandwich. It was the middle of the week and just enough past the busiest part of the tourist season that there were few other people on the beach, which suited him well. The fewer people he encountered, the better.

He stretched out on a chaise situated in a cabana on the pink sand and unwrapped both his sandwich and his laptop. Halfway through his sandwich, a young woman approached him from the Tiki bar to ask if he'd like to order a drink. He ordered his usual Rum Zizzle and asked her to bring him a second one in fifteen minutes.

She returned with his drink, which he paid for in cash along with a generous tip. She said she would return with his second one in fifteen minutes as requested.

Daniel sighed when she left. He sipped his drink as he finished his sandwich and opened his laptop. He wanted to check on his various accounts to have a better idea of his options for disappearing. He began to feel the relaxing effect of the rum and felt like he had managed a successful escape from the life he no longer wished to live. However, as he opened his first account online, he was shocked to see that it was empty. He checked the second account and found it empty, too. He downed what remained of his drink and began to panic. He picked up his cell phone to call Tori and ask her what was going on when he suddenly felt severe pain in his stomach. He put down his cell phone and rested his head on the back of the chaise hoping the pain would pass—that it was the unfortunate result of downing his drink along with a deli sandwich.

However, the pain grew worse. His mouth suddenly felt wet. He wiped his mouth with the back of his hand and was startled to see foam. Then he dropped to his side in the chaise, and everything went black.

# Chapter 11

McKenna felt the familiar anxiety begin to rise within her. She took a few deep breaths to calm it before it could become overwhelming.

"Captain Vick," she began.

"You can call me, Vick, Ms. Hollingsworth."

"Okay, Vick. And I'm McKenna."

Vick nodded.

"I need a few minutes with my sister alone," she continued.

Vick nodded again and gestured to Nadia to follow him into the kitchen, but McKenna remembered they had been able to hear Vick's part of the conversation with NSA from the dining room, so she took Mac by the arm and walked to one of the bathrooms and turned on the sink full blast. Mac smiled at her sister's creative effort for privacy.

"What's up?" she said.

"I don't want you to go, Mac. Someone's been trying to kill you, remember?"

Mac sat down on the edge of the bathtub, and McKenna sat on the lid of the toilet. "Yes, I realize that, but I think I'll be safe at NSA, don't you?"

"I don't know!" McKenna stood up and threw up her hands and began pacing back and forth in the small bathroom. "I don't know what to think anymore!"

Mac nodded and patted the edge of the bathtub. "I know," she said. "Please sit back down."

McKenna obliged, closed her eyes, and heaved a big sigh before looking at her sister again. "Okay. Maybe you'll be safe at NSA. I hope so. We're all that's left of our family." Mac nodded. "But what about me?" McKenna continued. "Am I going to be safe here? I mean, they've got people guarding me, too—those agents outside and that woman, Nadia, who is probably someone like Ziva David."

Mac smiled at her sister's reference to a character on her favorite TV show, NCIS, which the two of them had binge-watched together on a few of Mac's trips home. "Well, if she's anything like Ziva, I'd say you're in good hands. Wouldn't you?"

It was McKenna's turn to smile. "Are you really trying to comfort me by playing on my admiration of a fictional character?"

"Yeah," Mac said with a smile, "if it works."

McKenna ran her hand through her hair and nodded. "But what am I supposed to do here, Mac? And for how long?" She paused long enough that Mac started to answer, but then she added, "And how am I going to know that you're okay?"

"I don't know, Sis. I think they will do the best they can to let you know I'm okay. In fact, I'll insist on it." She gave McKenna's hands a small squeeze. "They often have to do brutal work, but that doesn't mean they're not caring people. Well, at least some of them are caring people."

"Some of them?" McKenna raised her eyebrows.

"Most of the ones I know are," Mac said.

"And you're one of them, aren't you? I mean, I know you're a caring person, but you sometimes have to do brutal work, too?"

Mac released McKenna's hands, stood up, and did a little pacing of her own. "I've had a little training, but I've been fortunate to not have to use it."

"But you would?" McKenna persisted.

Mac stopped pacing and sat back down. "If I had to, yes. It goes with the job, Kenna."

"The job of a French Horn player?"

The look on Mac's face told McKenna she had gone too far.

"No. It doesn't go with the job of being a French Horn player. It does, however, go with the job of being a member of the Navy on loan to the NSA."

They were both quiet for a few moments. Mac had visibly calmed down.

"Kenna, I didn't want any of this to happen, but it did. I'm doing the best I can. I just..." She hesitated. "I just need you to do the best you can with all of this, too. I know that's not fair, and I'm sorry, but it's where we are right now."

McKenna looked into her sister's eyes with tears in her own. "I know, Mac. And I'm sorry, too. Of course, I will."

They both stood and hugged each other.

"I love you, Mac."

"I love you, too." Mac turned off the water faucet as McKenna dried her tears with her sleeve. "Are we good?" she asked.

"Always," McKenna responded.

Mac laughed. "Well, not always! Remember that time when I..."

McKenna laughed, too, knowing only too well the memory Mac was about to recall. "No, let's not revisit *that* again!"

They exited the bathroom and made their way back to the dining room where they found Vick and Nadia waiting.

"Everything okay?" Vick asked.

"Yep, we're good," Mac said, "but please keep McKenna informed periodically that I'm safe."

"Will do," Vick agreed. "Let's roll."

* * *

Vick and Mac rode in silence as he drove the short distance from the safehouse in Laurel, MD, to NSA Headquarters near Fort Meade. They passed through the first security checkpoint at the gate, then the first security checkpoint inside, and then entered the elevator, where Vick swiped his ID card and pressed the button for Sublevel 3. As the doors opened, they were greeted by a man who looked too young to be there, but he *was* there, and that meant he was exactly where he was supposed to be. No one was on Sublevel 3 who didn't belong there. His ID badge displayed his name as Bill.

He ushered them past a large room filled with cubicles attended by other young people who were watching their large monitors. Large TV screens lined one short wall, each of them broadcasting news stations from around the world. Bill led them down a long hallway and opened the door for them to a large conference room. Then he closed the door behind them. Mac wondered if he was standing post outside the door or moving on to his next task but decided that it didn't matter. They were now in one of the most secure facilities in the world. She had been here before, and she knew she was safe here.

Three people were already sitting around the conference table. File folders and papers were splayed out in front of each of them. Mac recognized General Andrew Sullivan, Director of the National Security Agency and Chief of the Central Security Service; and Paul Clement, Deputy Director and senior civilian leader of NSA. However, she didn't recognize the third person sitting with them, a distinguished-looking woman who Mac guessed to be in her fifties. Her uniform identified her as an Army General.

Deputy Director Clement told the two new arrivals to sit down. "I believe you both already know Gen. Sullivan, and, of course, you know me." He gestured to the woman seated with them. "This is General Anna Schwartz. She is the commanding officer at the Army Medical Research and Development Command at Fort Detrick."

Both Vick and Mac nodded a greeting and said simply "General" before sitting down.

The conference room door opened again, and another familiar face entered. Vernon Jordan was head of Section 5, tasked with leading the investigation that had upended the lives of Mac and her sister.

"Generals," he said with a nod as he approached the table. "Good to see you again, Vick. It's been a while."

Vick stood, and the two shook hands. Vick sat back down, and Jordan turned to face Mac and sighed.

"And Mac," he said, almost but not quite apologetically, "here we are again."

Mac only nodded in acknowledgment.

"General Sullivan, may we begin?"

The general nodded. Mac realized there was a lot of nodding going on but very few words.

"With General Sullivan's permission," Jordan said. "I've asked General Schwartz to join us because she has information vital to this case. You, Mac, are here because of a recent development in the case that requires your participation." Jordan held out his hand in an invitation to speak. "General Schwartz?"

Without a word, Gen. Schwartz picked up a remote control, and what appeared to be a chemical formula appeared on one of the large monitors on the opposite wall. "Gentlemen—and Ms. Hollingsworth—this is the chemical configuration of the substance in the vial that was found inside a slide of Ms. Hollingsworth's French Horn."

"Anna," Gen. Sullivan sighed, "help us out, here. I don't think anyone in this room—other than you—has any understanding of what this means."

Schwartz looked down for a moment, and Mac thought she looked suddenly—something—what was it? Nervous? Do generals get nervous?

"Of course," she continued, looking back up. "What you are seeing is the formula for an agent we wish we had never created. It is 100% lethal. There is—at least at the moment—no known antidote or countermeasure. It can be aerosolized." She paused to take a breath. "And the effects that it has on the human body are contagious."

"We?" Clement seemed to almost spit out the question. "Are you telling us that 'we' means 'you' and your geniuses at Fort Detrick created this thing—in violation of treaty?"

"Yes, Mr. Clement. That is correct." A stunned silence permeated the room for a moment before she added, "I have already submitted my resignation to the Army Chief of Staff. His decision is pending, largely dependent on the outcome of this situation. He has asked me to remain at least until we resolve this crisis."

Vernon Jordan tossed his pen down on the conference table and looked first at Mac and Vick before turning toward Gen. Schwartz. "May I ask a question, General?"

"Of course."

"What is the action involved in its lethality?"

Schwartz looked at Sullivan, who chose to answer the question.

"I'm afraid that's classified, very compartmentalized information, Mr. Jordan. Let me just say this: It's our worst nightmare."

Mac's head was spinning. *Why am I here? Why are they including me in this disclosure?*

Gen. Sullivan seemed to read her mind. "You, Ms. Hollingsworth, are here because the man who attempted to smuggle this substance via your instrument has requested to speak with you. We have the vial you found. It seems he is in control of two others. We need your help retrieving those, but we wanted you to understand the level of danger involved."

"Has my command been informed?" she asked.

Sullivan nodded. "In general, to the degree that we feel prudent." He paused for a moment before asking in a surprisingly gentle voice, "Do you need a few minutes, Ms. Hollingsworth?"

Mac shook her head slightly. "No, sir. I'm in."

* * *

Back at the safe house, McKenna had tried in vain to distract herself by channel surfing. Finding nothing that interested her, she walked to the bookcase to peruse the collection of books, CDs, and DVDs in the hope of finding something compelling enough to take her mind off of all that had happened—and that was going to continue to happen for some unknown period of time. She found herself wondering what her protector, Nadia, was doing and wandered into the kitchen where she found her talking with one of the agents posted outside. They seemed to have ended their conversation as McKenna entered, and Nadia shut the door.

"Do you need something, Ms. Hollingsworth?" she asked as she locked the deadbolt on the door.

McKenna sighed. "Please just call me McKenna, okay? If we're going to be stuck here together, I think we can be on a first-name basis, don't you think?"

Nadia smiled. "Of course, McKenna. Is there something I can do for you?"

"I don't know." McKenna paused, glancing around the kitchen. "I guess I've got the munchies. Got any cookies in here?"

Nadia went to the pantry and returned with a bakery box of assorted cookies that all looked delicious. "Milk?" Nadia asked.

"No, I'm not much of a milk person. Coffee?"

Nadia stepped over to a Keurig coffee maker that sat on top of a small platform with a drawer. She opened the drawer and removed two coffee pods. "Regular or unleaded?"

McKenna laughed. It felt good to laugh. "Normally, this late, I would say unleaded, but I think I'll go for regular tonight." Then she surprised herself by asking, "Will you join me?"

"Sure, I can do that," Nadia replied with another smile.

McKenna had never thought about federal agent types smiling much, except maybe the ones portrayed on TV, but Nadia's smile seemed genuinely friendly—warm, in fact.

The two sat on bar stools at the kitchen island with their coffee and opened the box of cookies. McKenna selected a white chocolate, macadamia nut cookie and one with chocolate chunks. Nadia sipped her coffee for a few moments before also choosing a white chocolate, macadamia nut cookie.

"I know this is a comfort food thing," McKenna said sheepishly. "You know, sort of self-medicating with sugar." She tilted her head back for a moment and sighed. "But I'm willing to own that at the moment. It's been a hell of a day."

Nadia nodded. "I understand. You didn't ask for any of this. In fact, you probably could never have imagined the things that have happened to you in the past couple of days."

McKenna shook her head. "No, I couldn't have." She stared into her coffee for a moment as she chewed a bite of cookie. "My friend was killed—Annie. She was the one in Mac's car. I loved her. She was my best friend, but with all that's happened, I haven't even cried about her death—and, my God, she has children." She took a sip of coffee. "They have their dad, of course. I know him, too. He's a good father, so I'm glad they still have him."

"I'm sorry about your friend," Nadia said.

"Thank you. But what's even worse is knowing that the explosion was meant for Mac." McKenna shuddered. "I don't know how I would cope with losing her. We don't have any other family—only each other. Annie was family to me, though, and now she's gone. If I were to lose Mac..." She closed her eyes as she took a sip of her coffee.

"I don't think there are any plans that would put Mac in further danger, McKenna—not any that I'm aware of, anyway."

"Thank you for saying that, Nadia." McKenna smiled. "I'm not sure I really believe it, but I hope you're right." She paused as they both munched on their cookies and sipped coffee. "So what's your story, Nadia? How did you come to work for NSA?"

Nadia smiled again, and McKenna found herself strangely warmed by it. "It's not a long story, really," she said. "I joined the Marine Corps after college. A lot of people in my family had served in the Corps, so it felt important for me to do that, too. Because I had what they considered an 'interesting mix' of college courses, I wound up in Intelligence. I served six years in the Corps and then was recruited by the NSA. I've been with the Agency for a little over five years now."

"Wow," McKenna said, "I'm impressed—and honored that someone with your background is protecting me. Thank you."

"You're welcome."

"So do you have your own secret bunker like Agent Vick does?"

Nadia looked puzzled. "Secret bunker?"

"Yeah, he took Mac and me to it before coming here. It was weird. It looked like just a cement building in the middle of nowhere but had all this security stuff, computers, and all that. It seemed like it was his office or something."

Nadia's puzzled look turned into a frown. "McKenna, do you remember where this place was?"

"No, not really. I figured it was part of the NSA. Mac said she needed to make a secure phone call, and he said that was the most secure place he knew of." Then McKenna frowned. "It's funny, though, now that you ask. I live in Laurel, Maryland, and, somehow, I think this place might have been near Laurel. The NSA is next to Fort Meade, which is just down the highway. I wonder why he didn't just take us there?"

Nadia held up a finger as she pulled out her cell phone. "Give me a few minutes, McKenna. I need to make a phone call."

McKenna remained on her bar stool, stunned, as Nadia walked to another room to make her phone call. What just happened?

# Chapter 12

David had driven to Mac's apartment shortly after leaving the voicemail. He knew that once she, and the NSA, of course, heard the message, they were likely to stake out her apartment, and he didn't want to be arrested before having a chance to talk with her.

He parked several blocks away and walked to her apartment. It was 4:30 in the morning, so no one was around, and no cars were coming and going. Darkness has its advantages. His only concern was getting inside. One of his smuggling contacts had once shown him how to pick a lock. He was able to do it after the guy showed him, but he had never done it since. He never imagined he would have reason to break in anywhere. He was a smuggler, not a burglar or thief—well, he supposed many people considered him a thief because of his smuggling, but he told himself that although he didn't know where most of the things he smuggled came from, he didn't steal them himself. He also told himself that he had never hurt or killed anyone. He was beginning to realize those were rationalizations—rationalizations that had led to him getting in over his head.

He thought about the woman who had died in Mac's car—an innocent woman, a woman who left behind two children. He didn't even remember her name. He also knew the car bomb was meant for Mac. That wasn't his idea, but he had gone along with it in a desperate effort to try to protect himself, which he knew now was not only unsuccessful but stupid and reprehensible. Greed and jealousy were powerful demons that had seduced him to be an accessory to murder and attempted murder. He had never imagined he was capable of such horrific crimes—but here he was, not only capable but complicit—and guilty. He knew he deserved whatever punishment the criminal justice system imposed on him. He just hoped they got to him before Agma did.

He approached Mac's apartment door, pulled the lockpicking tools from his pocket, and hesitated. "Oh shit," he said softly to himself, "what if she has an alarm system?"

He tossed his head back in frustration and indecision. If she had an alarm system, and he set it off, he'd have to run. The chance to meet with her here would be gone. Then he remembered the night he had dropped her off. She'd unlocked the door, and they'd stood at the open door for a few minutes, talking. He didn't remember her disabling an alarm. Or did he?

He decided that, at this point, he had to make a decision. He thought the odds might be in his favor, but if he was wrong, he'd have to run and come up with some other plan to meet with her. He laughed at himself.

*Hell, screw the alarm problem. I'm not even sure I can get in.*

He worked the tools into the first lock and was successful. Then he worked on the deadbolt. It took him a little longer, but he finally heard it click. He took a deep breath and then opened the door. Silence. He let out his breath and slipped inside.

He walked from room to room in her small apartment. It suited her. There seemed to be so much of her present there. He noticed with a smile that there were horns of various kinds, made of various materials, which provided subtle clues to her love of the instrument. He had once had a similar collection.

Maybe all horn players did. He'd never been in another horn player's home before. There were a couple of framed posters, too. One was a French Horn with a bouquet of flowers emerging from its bell. He had seen that one before, but it wasn't his style. The other was more of a traditional Horn of Plenty, but the horn was a French Horn—with various fruits and vegetables emerging from its bell. He'd never seen that one before, but he liked it.

"Where did you find that one, Mac?" he asked, as if she were there to answer him.

He opened a few drawers in the desk in her bedroom. Most of them held pens, markers, paper clips, rubber bands, envelopes, and other desk-type supplies. Then he opened the top middle drawer and found a leatherbound book with a hunting horn embellished on the cover. He opened it expecting to find some horn-related information or notes, but what he found was what seemed to be a sort of diary or journal. He knew it would be an invasion of her privacy to read it and put it back in the drawer. As he started to walk out of her bedroom, though, his curiosity got the better of him. He went back and retrieved it from the drawer, then sat on her bed and flipped through it. He stopped at a page where he saw the name David. He wondered at first if she knew another David or was this about him? Then he began reading.

March 13, 2023

*I asked David if he wanted to get some coffee together and talk about our rehearsal. I've asked before, and he's always had some excuse, but I thought I would try again. He seems like a nice guy. I'm not interested in dating him or anything. I would just like to be friends. He had another excuse today for not joining me. Oh, well.*

He flipped through a few pages until he saw his name again.

April 4, 2023

*David brought me home tonight. I was surprised that he offered. I've made several friendly overtures to him over the years, but he just never responded. I decided that he didn't like me for some reason, and I guess I quit trying. It always bothered me, though. I wasn't close friends with everyone in the horn section, but I considered them all friends. We shared a comradery with each other. That is, everyone except David. He just seemed to not want to be a part of that for some reason. I've felt sad about that. We sit right next to each other for hours at a time at rehearsals and performances. I guess he has his reasons.*

*When he brought me home tonight, though, it seemed like something else was going on with him. He wanted to come in. I considered it, thinking maybe this was an opportunity for us to connect with each other, but it was so late, and I was so tired. I just didn't have it in me, so he left. It was so weird, though. A little while later, I went into the kitchen for a glass of water, and I noticed that his car was still parked outside. I'm not sure what to think about that.*

David flipped a few more pages, wondering if he would see his name again. He did.

April 11, 2023

*I don't think I've ever felt so angry and so betrayed. And the thing is, I can't even write about what's happened here. I wasn't sure how David felt about me, but I guess I know now. That's probably why he wanted to come in that night he brought me home. Damn.*

That was the last entry. It was brief, but he knew exactly what she was referring to. He knew it was written when she learned that he was the one who had placed the vial in her horn. She had probably also figured out he had been responsible for the attempts on her life.

He closed the journal and returned it to the desk drawer. He went back to the living room where he had left his backpack. He pulled a bottle of water out and took a long drink. Then he did something he hadn't done since he was a very young child. He sobbed. He sobbed until he fell asleep.

He woke up later with a start. *Oh, shit, I can't believe I've been asleep! What time is it?* He looked at his watch. It was already two P.M.. He had six hours before Mac was supposed to meet him here—and there were things he needed to do before she arrived.

# Chapter 13

Vick and Mac left the meeting at NSA after the discussion and agreement between their various bosses resulted in a plan of action. Mac was to enter her apartment alone but armed. Vick would remain outside but serve as backup if needed and would be listening in on her conversation with David, along with the small contingent of brass at NSA. The mission was for her to find out who was behind the plan that involved a deadly agent being implanted in her horn. Other operatives were on stand-by once this information was obtained, and they were charged with whatever action was necessary. Information about the next stage of the mission was compartmentalized. Vick and Mac weren't briefed on it at all. Vick seemed annoyed about being left out of that but concealed the annoyance during the briefing. Once he and Mac were alone in the car together, however, the tension was palpable.

"Is something wrong, Vick?"

"What?" Vick replied, seeming slightly startled by her question. "Why do you ask?"

Mac shrugged. "I don't know. I guess you seem more tense than I've seen you since this all started."

Vick dismissed her perception with a wave of his hand. "Just thinking through this plan, I guess— pretty normal pre-mission tension. I'm fine." He paused and then glanced at her. "How about you, Mac? How do you feel about meeting with this friend of yours?"

Mac frowned. "I wouldn't exactly call him a 'friend.' He did try to have me killed a couple of times."

"What do you think he wants to talk with you about?"

Mac was thoughtful for a moment. The bosses had asked her the same question after they all heard the voicemail David had left. She replied now as she had then. "I have no idea."

"You've known each other for a long time, though, right?"

Mac was annoyed that this conversation seemed to be covering the same ground that had already been covered during the meeting at NSA. "Yes," she said, with an air of finality. "We've known each other for years, but as I said in the meeting, David is a loner. Any overtures of friendship I or others have made to him have never been accepted."

After Mac had found and reported the vial hidden in her horn, NCIS had quietly investigated David but found no evidence of other suspicious activity, except that he seemed to suddenly disappear.

"The NCIS investigation found nothing. He seemed clean."

Mac felt like he was fishing for information that perhaps she had previously withheld. "Yeah," was all she said.

They rode in silence for a few moments before Mac decided to steer the conversation in another direction.

"So, this double role you play with NSA and Maryland State Police. How does that work exactly?"

Vick smiled. "It's unusual, I admit, and often difficult to navigate. It was an idea I had a few years ago that the higher-ups found interesting—you know, having their fingers in more than one agency pie, so to speak."

"Has it worked the way you envisioned?"

"At times." He didn't elaborate and seemed distracted.

"Are there other dual operatives like you?"

Vick smiled again. "Sorry, Mac, that's classified."

"That little bunker of yours must come in handy in both of your roles."

He didn't respond. Mac wasn't particularly digging for information. She was just trying to ease the tension in their conversation.

"It does, yes."

*Well*, she thought, *this is going nowhere. Maybe it's time to talk about something else.*

"I wonder how McKenna is doing back at the safehouse? Can we check on her and also let her know I'm okay?"

"Maybe we should wait until we know for sure," he replied. "We don't know what this guy wants to talk with you about or what tricks he may have up his sleeve."

"It would be good to touch base with her, that's all. She's been through a lot these past few days."

Vick took out his cell phone and clicked on his passcode before handing it to her. "Okay, but keep it short. We're almost there, aren't we?"

"Yeah, we are," she said, taking the phone.

"Nadia is on my list of contacts."

Mac took the phone, found Nadia, and pressed the call button. Nadia answered on the first ring.

"Hi, Nadia, it's Mac. Vick gave me his cell phone so I could check on McKenna. How's she doing? Can I talk with her?"

Nadia didn't immediately respond. When she did, Mac sensed something was wrong. "Where are you right now, Mac?"

"I'm with Vick in his car. We're..." She paused and glanced at Vick, who shook his head, reminding her their destination and mission were classified. "We're on our way to another meeting."

"Mac," Nadia continued in a much quieter voice, "listen to me carefully. We have reason to believe Vick may have his own agenda, but we're not sure what that is. Your sister mentioned he took you both to a private bunker. Mac, I've checked with our superiors. Vick has not been authorized to create such a location. He hasn't responded to calls or messages. We think you could be in danger with him. Backup is being sent to your apartment as we speak. Please contact us when it's safe to do so." Nadia ended the call.

Mac held the phone in her hand, trying to comprehend what Nadia had told her. She finally handed it back to Vick. "Thanks."

"So how is McKenna?" he asked.

"She's okay. Nadia said she was asleep, and she didn't want to wake her."

"Seems like it took her a long time to tell you that."

Mac stared out the car window as they neared her neighborhood. Vick pulled the car to the side of the road. When she turned to ask him what he was doing, he was pointing a gun in her direction.

"I think you need to tell me exactly what Nadia said to you."

# Chapter 14

Nadia returned to the bar stool in the kitchen where she had shared cookies and coffee with McKenna. How could she tell McKenna that Mac was likely in more danger than anyone had expected her to be? How could she tell her much of anything? Her conversation with the executive team at NSA had sent everyone into action in several different directions because no one seemed to have any idea what Vick's agenda was. Being unpleasantly surprised by one of their own was not unheard of at NSA, but fortunately, it didn't happen often. Lack of intelligence in such situations didn't usually last very long because, when General Sullivan ordered "All Hands on Deck," all hands tirelessly searched for information about the rogue colleague and, inevitably, would yield results.

While her colleagues at NSA scrambled for information, however, Nadia was left with the delicate task of protecting McKenna, and she knew McKenna wanted to know what was going on. If she had any doubt about that, the look on McKenna's face made it clear.

"McKenna, there's been a development."

"A development? What does that mean, Nadia? Is it a good development or a bad development?"

Nadia could hear the tension and anxiety in McKenna's voice.

"I'm afraid we're not sure just yet," Nadia offered. She took a sip of her now cold coffee and weighed her words carefully. "Vick is not answering his phone or responding to messages. The backup team is on its way to find out his status and determine what has caused the lack of communication. It may be something as simple as an equipment failure of some kind."

"Equipment failure? An NSA equipment failure?" McKenna responded incredulously. "I have a feeling that doesn't happen too often, Nadia." She leaned her head so she could look Nadia directly in the eye. "What's really going on?"

"We aren't sure at the moment, McKenna. I'm being honest about that. I'm also being honest when I say that when we know more about the situation, I'll tell you what I can."

McKenna closed her eyes, took a deep breath, and struggled to dial down her level of anxiety. Nadia observed her and waited. After a few moments, McKenna opened her eyes again, sat up, crossed her arms, and spoke with a new calmness and resolve.

"I know I'm not an agent, intelligence officer, or whatever else you all call yourselves, Nadia, but I can usually tell when someone is withholding information. I was told that I would be kept informed of what was happening with my sister."

Nadia nodded. "Yes, you were," she conceded, then took a deep breath of her own. "An equipment failure may be a possibility, but you're right—it's unlikely. I was puzzled and concerned when you told me about Vick's 'secret bunker,' so I called headquarters. No one there knows anything about it, but they do know that he was never authorized to establish such a place. That, coupled with his lack of communication since leaving headquarters, has raised the possibility that he has an unknown agenda. He may have gone rogue."

\* \* \*

McKenna studied her protector's face and found not only honesty, but also what seemed to be kindness there. "And what do you think this may mean for Mac?" she asked, although she was sure she knew the answer.

"It means we're uncertain about Mac's safety right now. I'm sorry, McKenna."

McKenna nodded as a frown formed on her tired face. "Thank you for being honest with me, Nadia."

Nadia touched McKenna on the shoulder. "We're doing everything we can, McKenna, but don't discount Mac, either. She's smart, and she knows how to take care of herself, don't you think?"

McKenna smiled. "Yeah, I've seen her do some things since all this started that I've never seen her do before." She reached up to pat the hand Nadia still had on her shoulder. As her hand touched Nadia's, McKenna felt a rush of energy run through her body—a rush she had never felt before. She turned to Nadia and opened her mouth to speak but found no words available.

Nadia smiled back. "Would you like some more coffee?"

* * *

Back in Vick's car, Mac told him what Nadia had said.

"Thank you. That's very helpful. I wasn't sure you'd be that forthcoming."

"We're a block away from my apartment where I'm supposed to meet a man who has tried to kill me—and, oh yeah, you're holding a gun on me, Vick."

"So I am. I was being cautious. I thought you might draw yours."

"It's still in the glove box, Vick. What's going on?"

"I'm not your enemy, Mac."

"And yet you're still holding a gun on me."

Vick withdrew the gun to his lap but kept his hand ready to draw it again if necessary.

"The goal of the mission remains the same, Mac. We know there are still two vials of that bioweapon out there somewhere. You're supposed to get David to tell you where they are, and you and I will retrieve them if possible."

"Okay," Mac said, glancing down at the gun in his lap. "The mission remains the same, but something has obviously changed. What is it?"

"What's changed is that when we get the vials, I take charge of them. They're not going back to NSA."

"Dare I ask what you plan to do with them?"

"I plan for them to fulfill their intended purpose."

"In the United States? You would do that to your own country? The country who you have sworn an oath to—several times, in fact—to protect?"

Vick shook his head. "Of course not. Don't be ridiculous. I'm a patriot, Mac. This weapon will be unleashed in North Korea."

"Oh, my God, Vick! And what do you think is going to happen when what's left of North Korea—and the rest of the world—sees that the United States has launched an unprovoked attack with such a deadly bioweapon?"

"Neither North Korea nor the rest of the world is ever going to think this weapon was unleashed by the United States. Everyone is going to believe North Korea did it to themselves."

"What?" Mac exclaimed. "How?"

"I've orchestrated it to appear that way from the very beginning. It's the reason all the other players in this deadly game believe in the plan. They believe it because they've never seen me or heard my actual voice, and they believe it because I go by the name of Agma—a Korean word for demon."

Mac was stunned—and momentarily speechless. She remembered hearing the name Agma in a briefing at NSA when she got pulled into all of this, but it didn't have much meaning to her at the time. She also remembered that everyone involved in the briefing believed Agma to be a North Korean intent on attacking the United States. No intel since then had suggested otherwise.

She finally found her voice again. "And you're telling me all this because... you plan to kill me?"

"Not necessarily. I'm not above it, but I'd prefer not to. I'd prefer your help."

"My help?"

Vick nodded. "I haven't been responding to command communications for a while—long enough that I'm sure they've concluded that something is wrong, especially since they've spoken to Nadia. I'm sure others will be converging on our location soon, so I need to get out of sight." He paused and took a deep breath. "I could kill you, abduct your friend David, and have him take me to the vials." He looked into Mac's eyes. "I'm sure I could persuade him to give them to me. It would be easier, however, for you to get him to take you to the vials and hand them over to you and you hand them over to me."

Mac matched his stare. "Why would I want to make any of this easier for you?"

Vick sighed. "Oh, Mac," he said in a tone of voice he might have used with a child. "You don't really want to die right now, do you? Your death would be meaningless. It won't change the outcome—and your sister would be left with no family at all."

Mac's mind was reeling, running through ideas that might lead to a way out of this mess and running through what the best response might be to what Vick had just said.

"I can almost see the wheels turning," he said with a chuckle. "But before you decide to try anything clever, remember that I will be listening to your conversation with David. And you will be able to hear me. If you do or say anything I don't like, I'll intervene—or one of my people will intervene. You will die, we'll take David, we'll get the vials, and we'll proceed with our plans. Do I make myself clear?"

Mac nodded. "Surely, you don't expect me to go in unarmed."

"No, of course not. Go ahead and take out your weapon," he said, again raising his gun in her direction.

Mac took her gun from the glove box, removed the clip to check it before reinserting it, and ratcheted it to put one in the chamber.

He handed her an earpiece. "Now go."

Mac pulled the door handle and hoped that once she was out, she could shoot Vick and wait for reinforcements—hopefully without getting shot herself. She stood on the edge of the road and closed the door as she drew her gun and prepared to fire. Vick was gone.

"Nice try, Mac," he said through the earpiece. "Now follow the plan before I change my mind."

Mac walked toward her apartment while thinking about how this was going to go. Vick hadn't killed her, but David might try to—again. This whole situation was crazy. She had been pulled into all of this because she found the vial in her horn and because those who outranked her believed she could be useful in somehow finding out from David what was in the vials and where the other two vials might be. Thanks to General Schwartz from Fort Detrick, they all already knew what was in them. They wanted Mac to help find them—not some specially trained black ops team or even a small group of agents to apprehend David and force him to reveal their location—her.

They had no intel on what contingency measures David might have made in the event of his capture or death. When he left the voicemail requesting to talk with her, they had unanimously decided she was their best bet. Her—a professional French Horn player in the Navy with a little self-defense and weapons training.

*Little is right*, she thought with a huff. *Much too little and probably much too late.* And yet, here she was.

She finally reached the door to her apartment and found it was locked. She wondered how David had gotten in.

*I guess he got a little extra training, too.*

She stood to the side of the door as she unlocked it, making sure she was out of David's line of fire—if that's what he had in mind. She heard Vick's voice through her earpiece again.

"No tricks, Mac. Remember, I'm listening."

"Yeah," she whispered back. "I remember."

She pushed the door open slowly and momentarily wondered what her neighbors would think if they saw her entering her apartment this way, but no neighbors were around to notice.

"Please come in, Mac," David said. "I'm not going to hurt you."

\* \* \*

Vick slipped from behind the large oak where he had avoided Mac's attempt to shoot him. Years of training and experience made his soundless move through the tree line effortless and unnoticed by the approaching black SUV he knew held the expected backup team from NSA. He waited as they pulled up behind his abandoned Crown Victoria until he saw the driver's door open and saw Tom Robertson emerge. He had worked with Robertson from time to time. Robertson was the person he had expected to be on this backup team. He was a highly intelligent and highly decorated Marine assigned to NSA three years ago.

Vick switched on his voice disguiser and changed the frequency on his communicator so Mac would not hear this conversation.

"Captain Robertson," said the electronic voice with a hint of a Korean accent.

Robertson stopped in his tracks, ducked behind the armored door of the SUV, and drew his weapon as he ordered the other members of his team to get down. "Who is this?" he demanded, searching the darkness around them and motioning the others to do the same.

"That is not important. Not now. What is important is that you and your team do not approach the vehicle in front of you. None of you would survive the explosion, and I have no wish to kill you. Nor do I wish to kill your friend Agent Vick, who has recently joined us."

"What the hell is this?" Robertson demanded more forcefully this time. "Who are you, and what do you want?"

"Your question is redundant, Captain, and that annoys me. I do not like being annoyed." The voice paused for a few seconds before continuing. "Good. Your silence suggests that you understand not to annoy me further. What I want is for you and your team to get back in your vehicle and return to NSA. Do not approach Ms. Hollingsworth's apartment and make no attempt to intercept her or Mr. Lindsay if one or both of them leave."

"I have orders to protect Ms. Hollingsworth," Robertson said firmly, "and I have no intention of disobeying those orders."

"Ah, how fortunate. My request will not cause you to disobey your orders. By doing as I say, you will indeed be protecting her, Captain. Ms. Hollingsworth is wearing two earwigs that have a unique design. They both contain a small amount of explosive that is under my control. Leave now, and she will remain unharmed. If you remain, however, I will not only detonate the explosive devices in her ears; I will also detonate the vehicle in front of you, which I assure you is armed with enough explosives that will either seriously disable or kill you and your team. If you choose the latter option, I'm afraid your friend Agent Vick will be killed as well."

"Shit."

"I expected something more eloquent from you, Captain, but your vulgar choice tells me you understand the situation. Please confirm that."

"Understood."

"Very well. You may leave now. And Captain..."

"Yes?"

"I will be watching."

"Understood."

Robertson ordered his team back into the SUV. As Vick watched them drive away, he saw Robertson bang his fist against the steering wheel. Then Vick tapped a number on his cell phone.

"Pick me up and give the order to clear the station. We've been compromised."

He then returned his communicator to Mac's frequency just as a gray van approached. The markings identified it as an Amazon Prime delivery van—something no one would find suspicious in any neighbor at almost any time of day or night. Robertson and his team didn't give it a second thought when it passed them going the opposite direction.

* * *

Jordan's cell phone rang and he recognized the number as Robertson's. "Robertson?" Jordan's voice was a combination of concern and confusion.

"Yes, sir. We have a problem." Robertson recapped what had happened when they reached Vick's Crown Victoria.

"And you just bought what he said?"

"Sir," Robertson carefully restrained his frustration. "This man hacked our communications. He shouldn't have been able to do that. His ability to do that gave me reason to believe the threats he made. What would you have us do, sir?"

Jordan took off his glasses, rubbed his eyes, and then ran his hand through what little hair he had. "Yeah, okay. I get that. Do you have any idea who this guy is?"

"No, sir. He was using an electronic voice disguiser. However, I did detect an accent. I'm not sure what kind of accent, but my guess is Chinese or maybe Korean—definitely an Asian accent, sir."

Jordan considered this information. "Oh, my God." He wondered if Agma himself or one of his people could have been the person Robertson had spoken with and who now had Vick in custody. "Asian..."

"I'm not sure, but I think so, sir. Your orders, sir?"

"Get back here. We're going to have to regroup and consider the best plan of action. I'll have our geeks check out your comms and see if they can learn anything more about this guy."

"What about Vick, sir?"

"Vick can handle himself, Captain," Jordan responded. *And if we get him back, he has a lot of explaining to do.*

"And Hollingsworth, sir?"

"Yeah," Jordan sighed, "Until we run this new information by our command, I'm afraid she's going to be on her own for a while."

"Understood, sir."

# Chapter 15

Mac slowly pushed open the door to her apartment with her weapon drawn and ready. She eased around the door and saw David sitting in the dining room she used as a practice room. His weapon pointed in her direction.

"You said you weren't going to hurt me, and yet your gun is pointing in my direction."

David placed his weapon on a nearby table. "I wasn't sure you'd come alone. I'm not going to hurt you, Mac."

"You've tried to kill me at least two times, David."

David nodded. "Yeah, I know. I'm sorry about that. I never thought things would go this far. I was wrong. I made a mistake."

"A mistake?" Mac said, appalled by his calmness and choice of words. "You killed an innocent woman, David—a woman who left two children behind."

David hung his head. "I know, Mac." He looked back up at her, and she noticed his eyes were red and swollen. "Mac, I just need to talk to you for a few minutes. Please."

Vick/Agma had been silent since she entered the apartment, but she suddenly heard him through her earpieces.

"Go ahead, Mac. Give him some rope. However, I'm not a patient man."

Mac ran her hand through her hair, pausing for a moment as if she could force her mind to come up with some way out of this situation. "Okay, David, but first, put your weapon over here on the coffee table—slowly."

David was still for a moment but then did as she asked. Mac motioned for him to return to the chair in the dining room. She holstered her weapon and walked to the refrigerator, opening it to retrieve two bottles of water. She handed one to David.

"Okay, I'm listening."

She pulled the magnetic dry-erase board from the front of her refrigerator that she used to remind herself of things to add to her grocery list. David tilted his head and began to ask what she was doing, but she held a finger to her lips to silence him.

She erased her notes of coffee, tea, and paper towels, and quickly wrote: *Don't comment on what I'm doing. Just talk.*

David frowned but nodded.

"I like your place, Mac. It looks like you," he said as he gazed around her apartment. "I used to collect horns, too." He smiled. "Maybe all horn players do. I don't know." He paused, but she motioned for him to continue. "I've had some of the same pieces you have. Kind of weird, huh? Not the posters, though." He gestured to the poster of the Horn of Plenty hanging in the dining room. "I've never seen that one, though. Where did you find it"

Mac stopped writing for a moment. "It was a gift from my sister," she said, then resumed writing.

"I've loved the French Horn since I was a kid," he continued. "I think, in some ways, it probably saved my life."

Mac stopped writing and looked at him. "How, David?"

"I had a hard time as a kid. Things weren't good at home and weren't much better at school. I just never seemed to fit in anywhere. Awkward, kind of shy, didn't have any self-esteem. You've known me for a while. I'm sure you get the picture."

He smiled, and their eyes met. David quickly looked away. "Anyway, there were times when I was so miserable, I thought about killing myself—until I discovered the horn." He closed his eyes. "When I first saw it and heard it, it just seemed magical to me somehow. I can't explain it. I guess it sounds corny, but it was like an almost spiritual experience." He opened his eyes.

"I don't think it sounds corny at all, David. It's been that way for me, too," she said softly.

"I've always been jealous of you, Mac. I think that's what keeps me from being friends with you—and I know you tried."

"Jealous? I don't understand, David. You're a professional horn player, too."

David shook his head. "Not like you are, Mac." He gestured around the practice area to all her books, her Silent Brass system, and her musical accessories. "I have most of the same things you do—the same books, same recordings, the same tools. But you have a mastery of the horn that has always seemed beyond me. How do you do it, Mac? What's your secret?"

Mac was stunned. "I don't have any secret, David. I've just always worked hard. I know you have, too, or you would have never made it into the Navy Band."

David shrugged. "I got my master's degree at Ohio State. You got yours at Peabody."

Mac shook her head. "I don't understand, David. You're a professional French Horn player. Do you realize how many horn players only dream of that? You've played with almost every Chamber Group in the Baltimore-Washington Metro Area. Where is this coming from?"

David smiled. "Old stuff, I guess." He paused for a few moments. "You know, when Bill retired as principal horn, I wanted that position—so did you and Art. All three of us auditioned, but you're the one who got it. No one can top you, Mac."

Mac opened her mouth to say something but realized she wasn't sure how to respond.

David continued. "My jealousy and frustration got me in trouble." He glanced at the Horn of Plenty poster. "I turned something I loved into a Horn of Plenty of a different kind. I used it to make money—a lot of money."

Mac finally spoke. "Your horn? Are you talking about the vial you put in my horn?"

David shook his head. "No. I smuggled things—diamonds mostly, but never anything like that." He sighed deeply. "I was planning to smuggle the vials in my horn one at a time. I had the first one with me one day in the band room when I noticed a couple of plain-clothes guys talking to Jamison. I found out later they were NCIS, and I got nervous. Guilty conscience, I guess," he said with a sad smile. "So when you left your horn to go to the bathroom before rehearsal, I removed a slide and stuck the vial in it. I thought I would retrieve it later, but that didn't work out."

Mac nodded. "You planned to retrieve it the night you drove me home."

"I'm sorry, Mac. I never meant for any of this to happen. I don't even know what was in that vial, but I was told it was deadly."

Mac heard Vick/Agma in her earpiece again.

"I was about to lose my patience with this very sweet conversation, but now we're getting somewhere. Find out where the other two vials are. The clock is ticking."

Mac took a deep breath and wrote again on the dry-erase board. Then she turned to face David. "David, are you crying?" She quickly nodded.

"Yeah, I guess I am."

Mac turned the dry-erase board toward him.

*Don't respond to this by talking. Agma is listening. I need to know where the other two vials are but write it down here. When I ask you where they are, lie about their true location. Do you have an unused burn phone? If you do, I need it now!*

David was shaking, and Mac noticed there were, indeed, now a few tears in his eyes. He looked terrified but finally nodded and pulled a burn phone out of the backpack at his feet and handed it to her.

She wrote on the board: *Talk—about anything.*

David was still shaking a little but started talking again. "I love my country, Mac. I don't know what's in those things, but I was told they were deadly. I knew I couldn't go through with this job."

As David talked, Mac texted Jordan's number.

*"This is Mac. Vick is Agma. He's listening, so text if you must, but DON'T CALL. Target is not US, it's North Korea. Will text you location of the other two vials soon."*

"I believe you, David, but we need to retrieve those vials. Where are they?"

* * *

Vernon Jordan looked at the text he had just received and then called General Sullivan. "General, there's been a new development we need to discuss, and I suggest, sir, that we do it in person as soon as possible."

"I'm on my way to the office right now. What's your ETA?"

"I can be there in fifteen minutes, sir."

"I'll have my aide gather the others."

"Very good, sir."

\* \* \*

David considered Mac's written direction about not mentioning the true location of the vials out loud. If Agma was really listening, he needed to make the lie convincing, and it needed to require his involvement, or he was as good as dead once he revealed it. He figured he was probably as good as dead anyway, but he didn't want to die knowing he might be able to prevent a terror attack on his own country.

"The other two vials are in a safety deposit box in Laurel, Maryland."

He took the marker from Mac's hand and wrote on the board: *They're in a safe in my home.*

Mac took the board back and quickly wrote: *Location?*

David shook his head. *No address. Catoctin Mountains.*

He wrote down the GPS coordinates, and watched as Mac texted Jordan both the lie and the truth.

\* \* \*

Vernon Jordan joined General Sullivan and his deputy chief, Paul Clement, in the conference room on Sublevel 3.

"General Schwartz is in a meeting with the President's National Security Advisor and won't be joining us, so tell us about this new development," Sullivan began. "It better be good."

"Yes, sir," Jordan said. "I think it might be."

"Might be?" Sullivan was indignant.

Jordan projected Mac's messages on one of the large screens on the wall.

Sullivan threw his pen down on the table. "What the hell is this, Jordan?"

"I'm not entirely sure what to make of it, sir, but I think we need to move on this information as quickly as possible."

"Vick has worked with us for years," Clement said. "He's never given us any reason to question his loyalty or his patriotism."

"Yes, sir," said Jordan, "that's true. I've worked with him myself several times." He took a deep breath before adding, "We have, however, recently discovered that he has established some sort of secret bunker—something we didn't authorize. My attempts to reach him in the field have been unsuccessful."

"But the call you received from Agma indicated they have him. I wouldn't expect you to be able to reach him if he's in enemy custody."

Jordan nodded. "That's true, sir."

There was a moment of silence before Sullivan said, "What about Hollingsworth, Jordan? She hasn't been part of this for very long. What if she's more involved than we know? What if this is some misdirection on her part?"

Jordan was aghast. "Sir, are you suggesting Hollingsworth is somehow responsible for all of this?"

"Not necessarily," Sullivan conceded, "but how do we know?"

"Sir, she's been a French Horn player in the Navy Band for years. It's the only MOS she's ever had."

"That would be a good cover, don't you think?" Clement asked.

Sullivan reviewed his notes briefly. "This David Lindsey. She's known him and worked with him for several years. What if she's been involved with this from the beginning?"

"Gentlemen, Hollingsworth was fully vetted when we brought her into this thing. Her record is exemplary. There's nothing questionable in her background to support what you're suggesting. Then there's her parents..."

"Perhaps," Sullivan said, "but assumptions are dangerous things." He paused for a moment. "We're going to deploy two teams. One team will fly out to Catoctin, and the other will track Hollingsworth. Either way, we've got to get our hands on those vials."

# Chapter 16

McKenna woke up and was momentarily confused about where she was. Then the events of the past couple of days came back to her. She was surprised that she had even been able to sleep but being sleep-deprived during the course of these surrealistic events had finally caught up with her, in spite of all the coffee she had consumed with Nadia the night before.

Nadia. What was it about her? There was an attraction there McKenna had never experienced before. She wanted to be with her, to be near her, and wanted to touch her. Where was that coming from? McKenna hadn't dated until she went to college, and even then, there were only a couple of guys who interested her. Interested was the best word, she decided, because she couldn't say she had been sexually attracted to any of them. However, she married one of them, and when the marriage ended after only a few years, McKenna began to think of herself as asexual. She just didn't experience attraction to anyone. Sex wasn't important to her, and she wondered why it seemed so important to so many other people.

The billions of humans on the planet, however, were evidence that it was indeed important to a lot of people. She always thought there may be something missing in her—not something *wrong* really. She didn't feel like there was anything wrong with her. She just knew she was somehow different, and she was okay with that. At least she had been okay with it until she felt that spark of sensual energy when Nadia touched her on the shoulder. She wondered if Nadia had felt it, too.

There had been a particular look on her face that suggested she might have, but neither of them commented on it. Maybe it was just one of those things people experience once in a while but never happens again, and they're never sure that it really meant anything. Maybe it really didn't happen. Maybe it was... what?

She had been through a lot in the past couple of days, and most of it stirred up a host of emotions—anxiety, confusion, fear. Most of those feelings seemed to go from zero to one hundred very quickly. Maybe the unnameable feelings she had experienced with Nadia were part of all that. It would make sense. It was important to her that things in her life made sense. She concluded that must be it, and the conclusion provided the motivation for her to climb out of bed, put her jeans and sneakers back on, and head to the kitchen for a cup of coffee. The first cup in the morning was, without a doubt, one of life's simple pleasures.

When she got to the kitchen, Nadia was nowhere in sight. Agent Martinez was there, however. He had been one of the agents stationed outside for a while when they first arrived.

"Good morning," he said with a smile.

"Good morning," McKenna replied. "Where's Nadia? Did she leave?"

"No, she'll be back on duty soon. I understand she was up quite late last night. I came in early so she could get a few hours of sleep. We sometimes don't get enough of that in this kind of work."

McKenna got a cup from the cupboard, placed a pod in the Keurig, and stretched her arms and back as she waited for it to brew.

"Yoga?" Martinez asked.

McKenna laughed. "No, nothing as formal as that. I just find it helpful to stretch a little while I wait for my coffee." When her coffee finished brewing, she removed the pod, threw it away, and reached for her cup for that first-morning sip. The cup had almost reached her lips when Nadia walked into the kitchen.

"Good morning, you two. Getting acquainted with our charge, Martinez?"

McKenna's hand shook, and she spilled coffee down the front of her shirt and on the floor. "I'm sorry. I guess my hand slipped," she said, reaching for the roll of paper towels.

"Are you okay?" Nadia asked. "That had to be hot!" Nadia bent over to dry off the floor while McKenna dried off the counter.

The intensity of the energy in the room was suddenly palpable. Martinez looked at McKenna then at Nadia. He raised his eyebrows in an unspoken question.

Nadia shrugged. "No problem," she said. "We'll get this cleaned up and fix you another cup. I could use one myself."

McKenna had dried off the counter and was looking down at her shirt, which was now not only wet but also stained with coffee. "This is the only shirt I have with me."

"I have some clothes in my go-bag. I'm sure I have something that will fit you. You're welcome to it until we can get more of your things here."

Nadia left the kitchen, but McKenna just stared after her. She felt like her feet were stuck to the floor.

Nadia finally turned to her and said, "Come on, come with me."

McKenna finally managed to make her feet move and dutifully followed.

Martinez smiled, shook his head, and took another sip of his coffee.

\* \* \*

Mac turned the dry-erase board toward David again.

*I'm taking this with us because we may need it to communicate. I'm going out on a limb here, but I want you to take your weapon with you. Hide it but keep it close.*

David nodded and wrote: *I'm not going to shoot you, Mac. I want to make this right however I can.*

Mac wrote back: *I'm not going to shoot you, either, but we have to make this look like I might.*

David nodded. Mac clipped the marker to the dry-erase board, slipped it under the waistband of her jeans, and pulled her T-shirt over it. She picked up her weapon, keeping it in her hand so it would appear to anyone watching that she was covering David.

"We need to leave now," Mac said. Then she heard Vick/ Agma in her earpiece again.

"It's about time. Don't try anything clever, Mac. It won't end well for you."

"Understood," was all she said. David looked puzzled, so Mac pointed to her earpiece.

Mac gave David her key and had him lock her door, then took the key back and motioned him to stay in front of her. "We're going to that black car parked on the side of the road, two blocks ahead on the right."

They reached the car, and Mac told David to take the driver's seat. She slipped into the passenger seat and took a deep breath. She had no idea what exactly was going to happen when they got to David's safety deposit box and came out without the vials, but she knew it wouldn't be good. She wished David had chosen a fake location farther away to give her more time to think. Laurel wasn't far away. However, she was guessing the bank didn't open until at least 9 A.M., and it was only eight. That would buy her at least some time to think. David must have been having similar thoughts.

"Mac, my bank doesn't open until nine," he said. "What are we going to do?"

"Is there a drive-through place to get coffee near your bank?"

"Yeah, there's a Dunkin' Donuts and a McDonald's. No, wait, the Dunkin' Donuts doesn't have a drive-through."

"So let's go to McDonald's. We need to stay in the car until we get to the bank." Mac heard Vick/Agma in her earpiece again.

"McDonald's? Coffee?" he said, irritation clear in his voice. "What the hell are you doing, Mac?"

"Look," she responded with equal irritation. "You just heard him say that the bank doesn't open until 9 A.M.. So we're going to have a cup of coffee and wait until they open. What would you have us do, break in? I don't think that would get you what you want."

Vick/Agma sighed. "Very well. Enjoy your coffee, but I want you both at the bank when it opens at nine."

"Understood," was all she said.

While David drove, Mac texted Jordan.

"*David and I are on our way to the fake location. Agma says we're being watched, and I know he's following us. I'm leaving this phone on, hoping you can track us and send help. I'm not sure what to do when we come out empty-handed.*"

As she waited for Jordan to respond, she decided conversation might ease at least some of the tension. "David, why did you tell me all of that back at my apartment? It just doesn't seem like the David I've known for you to share such personal stuff."

"Well, you're right. It wasn't the David you've known." He paused for what seemed a long time, long enough that Mac opened her mouth to try to move the conversation forward, but then he responded in a voice strained with emotion. "Everything changed the day I was given those vials. This was no longer about smuggling diamonds and stuff and making money. This was something evil. Then that woman was killed—and it was supposed to be you. I felt evil being a part of it. I knew I was in over my head, but I didn't know what to do. Agma called me himself and told me I had two days to deliver the vials, or there would be consequences. I was scared. I still am." He turned to face her and added, "I don't expect to survive this situation, Mac. If Agma doesn't kill me—or have me killed—I'll go to prison for the rest of my life. I don't want to do that." He paused again. "Anyway, I didn't want to die with you or anyone else thinking I would betray my country."

"So are you saying, if Agma or one of his people don't kill you, you're going to kill yourself?"

Mac heard Agma in her earpiece again.

"That's a stupid question, Mac. He won't have the opportunity. He's a dead man, and he knows it—collateral damage in this engagement."

Mac was indignant. "Engagement? We are not at war with North Korea!"

Agma's response was equally indignant—and dismissive. "Of course, we are!"

David looked confused, so Mac pointed at her earpiece again.

Mac anxiously looked at David's burn phone and noticed she had finally received a response from Jordan. The response, however, was not what she had hoped for.

*"Yes, we're tracking you. Backup will come in right behind you as soon as you get wherever you're going. Another team is on its way to the coordinates you provided. Be advised. Your role in this situation is in question—not by me, but by others. Proceed with that information in mind. You may be treated as a hostile by the backup team."*

"Oh, my God," Mac said out loud without meaning to.

Vick/Agma assumed her comment was in response to his. "We've been at war with North Korea for years, Mac. They just didn't realize it, and, unfortunately, neither did our country." He was angry with her apparent naivete and continued his tirade. "Your parents tried to stop this mission years ago. They didn't know everything, but they knew too much. I couldn't allow them to learn anymore."

Mac's attention quickly shifted from her present danger to her past. "My parents died in a plane crash."

"Yes." Vick/Agma's tone was dark and strong. "But it wasn't an accident. There was a bomb on their plane."

Mac felt like all the air had been sucked out of her body. "I don't... They never told us there was a bomb on the plane."

"Well, of course, they didn't, Mac. You're new to this clandestine stuff, but I know you're smart enough to know that none of the three-letter agencies share everything they know."

"You killed my parents," she said, almost to herself.

"I did. They were getting too close. You can ask Jordan about the bomb—that is if you live through this. Maybe he'll even tell you the truth. There's a first time for everything." He paused, then casually added, "Enjoy your coffee."

# Chapter 17

David continued driving, puzzled by hearing only one side of the conversation Mac seemed to be having with Agma. He heard enough to understand why the life seemed to drain out of her. He pulled into the McDonald's drive-through.

"Do you still want coffee, Mac?" he asked softly.

She nodded as she stared absently out the front window of the car. David ordered two medium coffees with three cremes and sugars on the side because he didn't know how Mac took her coffee and didn't feel like this was the time to ask. He paid at the first window and at the next window picked up the coffees, then pulled into a parking space in the back, facing a large oak tree.

* * *

Emma Bateman unlocked the door to the Laurel Bank & Trust, entered, and locked the door again. It was eight. Employees wouldn't start arriving until at least 8:30 A.M., and the bank didn't open for business until nine, but Emma always came in early. It was important to her that everything was in order and ready for business. She walked through both customer and employee areas and was relieved to find all was well. She stopped by the employee breakroom and made herself a cup of coffee, then made her way to her office to review the order of her coming day.

As she took her first sip of coffee, she remembered it had been an acquired taste but had become something she now enjoyed. The window in her office provided a view of several trees—some young and some very old. She wondered which one of the old ones was the Mother Tree—a larger, older tree that nurtured the younger ones. She had recently learned that Mother Trees existed by reading a book about them. It warmed her heart to know they existed.

Emma's early life did not include any nurturing presence. She was born into a poor family in Rwanda who struggled to survive. She was the fourth child among eight. Life was hard—and then there was the war, the chaos, the killing. Her entire family had been murdered, and she had seen glimpses of it happening as she dared to peek through the thick cover at the very top of an old tree next to her home. She had climbed that tree many times but had never climbed it faster than she did that day. That tree had been a Mother Tree for her. It saved her life.

Many hours later, when the horror sounds gave way to an even more horrible silence, she saw a familiar vehicle approaching and waited to see who emerged before she climbed down. She was relieved to see it was a man she had seen before in her village. The only things she knew about him were that he was an American, had a kind face, often provided medical care in her village, and everyone called him Dr. B. She ran to him, and Dr. Bateman opened his arms to embrace her. Neither of them spoke, but a new life began for her that day.

Dr. Bateman and his wife adopted her at the age of twelve. She'd been named Keza at the time. They took her back to the United States and saw that she got the care she needed. With the unwavering love and support of her adoptive parents, Keza learned to trust. With the help of three different therapists who specialized in working with survivors of war, she learned ways and tools that helped her cope, but healing never really seemed complete. However, she excelled in school and was grateful for the life she had. As she approached her eighteenth birthday, her parents asked her what she wanted.

Keza asked if she could change her name. She felt like the name Keza kept her tied to the past, and she wanted a new name for her future. They were surprised at her request but told her they would take care of the legalities involved. Keza knew her grandmother, mother of her adoptive mother, was named Emma. She loved her grandmother, and she liked that name. Keza Bateman became Emma Bateman on her eighteenth birthday, and Emma felt like a new chapter had opened in her life.

It hadn't been easy, but Emma had gradually made her way in the world of finance. She was now the Vice President for Client Affairs, and it was rumored she would be named President of Laurel Bank and Trust when her boss, Michael Cohen, retired in six months. She smiled at that thought.

One of the keys to Emma's success at the bank had been her handling of its largest depositor, David Lindsey. Emma had gone out of her way to develop a business friendship with David, and her efforts had resulted in him entrusting the bank with more of his money and investments. She had a feeling he had much more money in banks outside the U.S., but that was never a topic of conversation between them.

Emma's memories that started with her admiring the trees outside her window ended, and she turned back to her desk to review her calendar. It was going to be a busy day. Employees would be arriving soon, so she started to leave her office when her business cell phone rang. It was her favorite customer.

"Hello, David. My, you are starting early today!"

"Yeah, I guess I am." He paused a moment. "Emma, are you in the office today?"

"Of course. I'm here now. What can I do for you, David?"

"I'm coming by at nine to get into my safety deposit box, and I would like for you to help me with that."

Emma was puzzled. David had been to the bank many times and knew there was another employee who usually handled safety deposit box visits. Why was he asking specifically for her? She considered that question only briefly before deciding he must have his reasons. Maybe he wanted to have a casual visit with her. It had been a few months since he'd been in.

"Of course, I will. I will be watching for you at nine."

"Thank you, Emma. I'll see you soon."

As Emma ended the call, a chill ran up the back of her neck, and she felt a familiar but unexplained sense of foreboding. She shook her head and looked around her office, relying on some of the grounding techniques she had learned in therapy using her five senses for times when she felt triggered. She counted the green items in her office. She rubbed the leather of her handbag. She put a peppermint in her mouth. She slipped off her shoes and rubbed her toes on the carpet in her office. She told herself that she was a Vice President with Laurel Bank and Trust and that she was safe. The feeling calmed down a little, but a remnant of it remained. Emma slipped her shoes back on and left her office to unlock the front door for her employees and to watch for David.

* * *

Mac wrote on the dry-erase board and turned it toward David. *Who's Emma?*

He wrote back: *VP at the bank. Has been friendly with me. She's a good person, and she will make sure the people in the bank are somewhere safe.*

Mac nodded and took another long sip of her coffee. David's friend at the bank might be able to keep the rest of the people in the bank safe, but she wasn't sure at all how she and David could remain safe, especially when Vick/Agma found out they had led him on a wild goose chase. She only hoped the team of federal agents Jordan was sending would get there before that happened. She heard Vick in her earpiece again.

"You two are very quiet, especially given all the intimate information that's been shared. What's going on?"

Mac responded, her tone edgy and agitated, "I don't know what you expect to hear, Vick. I just learned that you killed my parents. That information is hard to sit with. What we're doing is drinking our coffee and getting ready to go to the bank so you can have your damn vials."

"Right," Vick responded. "Just remember Mac—no tricks."

"Yeah," she said. "No tricks."

David looked at her but couldn't say anything. He pointed at the clock in the car, indicating the bank would open in five minutes.

She nodded. "Ok, let's go."

David didn't start the car, though. He reached into one of his pants pockets and removed an envelope. He handed it to her. The envelope was sealed, but on the front of it was written: *Read later.*

She frowned and wrote a question mark on the dry-erase board.

David just shook his head and wrote: *Just read it later.*

He started the car and circled the strip mall, stopping in front of Laurel Bank & Trust.

Mac wrote quickly on the board: *I'm taking my weapon—concealed. You do the same. If the backup team doesn't get here in time, we may need them.*

David did as she instructed. Then he took the board, erased it, and wrote: *(For Emma): Please don't speak out loud about this note. A dangerous man has followed us, and he is listening. He wants something I have. Federal agents are on their way to intercept him. Please quietly get everyone to the basement. I don't want anyone to get hurt.*

They both got out of the car and fell in behind a small group of customers getting ready to enter the bank.

Mac noticed one of the security guards hurrying to get to the front of the bank.

"Good morning, Mr. Lindsey," he said in a breathless voice. "I'm running a few minutes late this morning."

David smiled and said, "We all have those days, I'm afraid, Peter."

"Do you know *everyone* who works here?" Mac asked.

He shrugged "I know many of them. I have a sizable account here, and that tends to get a little extra attention sometimes."

Mac watched as a tall, professional-looking woman unlocked the front door, and customers formed a line for teller assistance.

"David!" the woman said as the other customers passed through. "It's so good to see you! It's been a while." She turned to Mac and asked, "And who is your lovely friend here?"

David gave the woman a casual hug, and Mac heard him whisper in her ear, "We need to go to your office." Then he added, "I wanted you to meet my friend, MacKenzie."

"Of course, of course," she said, taking Mac's arm as she led them down the short hall. "Welcome, MacKenzie!"

Once in Emma's office, they both took seats in front of her desk, and Emma perched on the edge of her desk.

Mac elbowed David, and he handed Emma the board. She started to ask what it was, but both David and Mac put their index finger to their lips and shook their heads. As Emma started to read what David had written, Mac saw her expression gradually change from one of happiness and joy to a frown of concern and fear. Her whole body seemed to freeze, and she stared straight ahead at the wall. Mac noticed Emma's body was shaking, and beads of sweat appeared on her forehead despite the chill from the air conditioning in the building.

"Em," David said, gently touching her arm. "Are you okay?"

David's touch seemed to bring her back to the present moment.

"Yes," she said, putting her hand over his. "Let me touch base with the tellers before I take you to your safety deposit box. Come out to the floor with me if you like and have a seat. It won't take me long." The tone of her voice was normal and clear with no evidence of distress. She pointed to the message on the board and nodded her understanding.

Emma led the way back down the short hall and motioned to two seats in the main area of the bank. David and Mac sat down, both nervous and uncertain about what might happen next. They watched as Emma entered the teller area and whispered in the ear of each of the four tellers on duty. All four were visibly shaken by whatever she had said, but each of them seemed to be shutting down their workstations. Emma then exited the teller area and repeated her whispers to the six confused customers standing in line.

As the tellers were leading customers to the basement, Emma went to the front door and asked Peter to come in for a moment. When he did, Emma locked the door and then whispered to him, too. Peter looked concerned by what she had said but made his way to the basement without asking any questions. Mac noticed that Peter was armed and wondered if he had ever had to draw his weapon at work. She hoped he wouldn't have to draw it today.

# Chapter 18

Vick and his crew of six were positioned at various points around the bank in teams of two, hidden by cars, trees, and dumpsters, but with clear views of the bank as they watched and waited. Dwight Holmes, Vick's second in command, sat with him in the BGE-labeled van on the opposite side of the parking lot, scanning the front door of the bank with binoculars.

"Boss, something strange is going on."

Vick squinted his eyes but finally took the binoculars from Dwight. "What do you mean 'strange?'"

"A couple of things, sir. First, I use this bank. I've seen that guard probably hundreds of times. His post is outside by the front door. He never goes inside. Second, and I could be wrong, but I think a woman may have locked the door after he went in."

Vick struggled to view what might be happening beyond the glass doors of the bank, but glare from the sun suddenly hit the doors. All he saw was light so bright, he had to put the binoculars down. He spoke into Mac's earpiece.

"What's going on in there, Mac? What's taking so long?"

"What do you mean 'what's taking so long'? We just got here, Vick. The bank just opened. The bank person helping us had a couple of things to do before she took us to the safety deposit box."

Vick turned off the speaker for Mac's earpiece and picked up his team radio. "Teams, report."

"Alpha team, sir. Nothing to report."

"Beta team, sir. Nothing to report."

"Kappa team, sir. The only thing we've seen is Lindsey and Hollingsworth in the office of a Black woman for only a few minutes before they all walked back to the front."

"And you're just now telling me this?" Vick's anger was evident. "What were they doing while they were in her office?"

"Unknown, sir. It looked like they were just talking, but you would have heard them through Hollingsworth's earpiece. The woman was sitting on the edge of her desk facing them, and all we could see was her back."

Vick thought back to what he had heard of their conversation. He remembered David asking the woman, Emma, if she was okay. That seemed strange to him, but he hadn't asked Mac about it at the time.

"Alpha team, sir. Something's going on. All the tellers and the guard are moving customers toward a door, but we can't tell where it leads."

*Somewhere safe*, Vick thought. *But how had Mac alerted the woman that there might be danger?* He had heard everything that she, David, and the woman had said.

"I don't know what you're up to, Mac, or how you communicated a danger without me knowing about it, but it was unnecessary. I had no intention of harming any of those people. I have, however, grown quite tired of your interference."

"I've done everything you told me to do," was Mac's only response.

"Right," he was his terse response. He handed the binoculars back to Dwight and got out of the van.

"What's up, boss?" Dwight asked with a mix of surprise and confusion.

"Stay here." He picked up his radio. "All teams. I'm going in. Maintain your positions until I say otherwise. Acknowledge."

Each team acknowledged.

Vick walked across the parking lot and up the few steps to the front doors of the bank. He knocked on the door and held up his Maryland State Police badge. His knock on the door drew the attention of the only three people who remained in the front part of the bank: Emma, David, and Mac. Emma walked toward the door to look at the badge more closely.

She started to unlock the door but stopped when David shouted, "No, Em! Don't let him in! He's the man we warned you about!"

Emma slowly stepped back away from the door and moved toward David and Mac.

Mac heard Vick's voice again in her earpiece. "Let me in, Mac. Once I have the vials, I'll be on my way."

\* \* \*

Mac looked at David. She was trying to decide what to do or say next. Suddenly, she took David's phone and quickly texted Jordan.

*"Do you have the vials yet? Agma is here. We are in danger."*

She didn't know if or when he might answer, but she was surprised when she saw his response almost immediately.

*"Vials are in custody. Team should arrive your location any moment."*

Mac let out a breath she didn't realize she had been holding. Maybe things would be okay. Maybe if she could buy a little more time, the backup team would arrive, and this would be over.

Her momentary hopes ended when she saw Vick draw his weapon. He shouted out to Emma.

"Ma'am, I don't know what these two have told you, but I am with the Maryland State Police. Open the door, or I will enter by force."

Emma looked at David and Mac, who both shook their heads.

"No, Emma," Mac said. "This man may have a badge, but he is not here as an officer of the law. He is dangerous. Please believe me."

Emma looked to David, who added, "She's telling the truth, Em. Don't let him in."

Their assurances were met with the sound of gunfire and breaking glass as Vick worked to enter the heavy glass doors, which were now broken but still impassable. He was struggling with the doors when sirens wailed and a voice spoke through a megaphone. The silent alarm had successfully reached the Laurel Police. Four police cars faced Vick at the front doors of the bank.

"Laurel Police! Put down your weapon and turn around slowly with your hands up!"

Vick put his gun down and raised his hands. "Maryland State Police!" he shouted back. "I'm going to pull out my badge."

Several guns were aimed in his direction. "Do it slowly!" the officer with the megaphone commanded.

Vick nodded. He reached into his jacket and slowly pulled out his badge.

"Toss it!" the voice commanded.

Vick tossed his badge and put his arms back up.

The officer with the megaphone motioned for the officer nearest Vick to retrieve the badge as the other officers kept their guns on Vick. The officer slowly moved toward Vick's badge, picked it up, and took it to the officer with the megaphone. All weapons remained on Vick while the officer put his megaphone down and examined Vick's badge. Then he lifted the megaphone again.

"Captain Vick, you may lower your hands but keep them where I can see them. You have to admit this is an extremely unusual situation. I'm going to have to take you in so we can understand what's going on here."

"I'm afraid I can't do that, Officer. This is a matter of national security." Vick pressed his jaw against his radio. "All teams. Fire!"

The police gathered around the front of the bank suddenly found themselves in a shoot-out from several directions. In the confusion of the surrounding gunfire, Vick picked up his weapon and used his body to push through the most damaged door.

He faced David, Mac, and Emma, with small cuts around his face and head. Out of the corner of his eye, he saw the dry-erase board lying on one of the chairs. "Clever," he said, looking at Mac. "But your cleverness has caused enough trouble, just like your parents before you." He pointed his gun directly at her. "Your services are no longer needed. Drop your weapon."

Mac was tired of having guns pointed at her. She had never had that happen until the past few days when all this started, and then it had happened several times. She knew the shot would kill her, but she was more angry than afraid. "Have you noticed how quiet it's gotten outside, Vick?"

He shifted his weight, and the gun lowered a little.

"That would be because NSA has a backup team outside, and I suspect by now that your team members are either wounded, dead, or under arrest. It's over. The vials aren't even here. They're in NSA custody. You've failed—Agma."

Vick raised his gun again. "Then I have nothing to lose."

David yelled, "No!" He jumped in front of Mac and pushed her away.

She was on the floor only a few feet from where she had dropped her gun. She watched as blood covered David's midsection, and he staggered back against the wall.

"David!" she cried, reaching for him, and he fell on the floor beside her.

"Convenient," Vick said. "It was time to get rid of him, too." He aimed his gun back toward Mac. "We haven't failed. Many others will follow. Goodbye, Mac."

There was a sound of a gunshot, but Mac realized that she hadn't been hit. Vick was falling backward with a surprised look on his face. In the chaos, Emma retrieved Mac's gun and shot Vick. She stood straight and tall with her feet slightly apart, the gun still held tightly with both of her hands, which were shaking.

Vick tried to raise his gun to fire back, but the bullet had found its way to his carotid artery. He couldn't fire back, he couldn't speak. There was a strange gurgling sound as he bled out, no longer a threat to anyone.

Mac walked over to him and kicked the gun from his hand. Emma had put down Mac's gun and was kneeling on the floor over David, who was still somehow alive. She held his hand and spoke softly to him, telling him that help was on the way.

David slightly shook his head and managed to say, "You saved us, Emma. Thank you." Then he lost consciousness.

* * *

Before Mac and Emma could process what had happened, NSA operatives in body armor and carrying automatic weapons filled the room. Four of them methodically cleared the area while one kept his weapon focused on Mac. Jordan walked in and immediately checked on the status of both Vick and David. He stood up and spoke to the team commander.

"That one's gone," he said, motioning toward Vick. "Lindsey is in bad shape, but alive."

"Very well," the commander said. "I'll inform Chief Hamilton. We need to get Lindsey to the hospital—with an armed guard," he stipulated. "And we need to get our forensics team in here." He nodded toward Mac and Emma. "What about them?"

"We need them both taken to NSA for questioning. Can you spare one of your guys to accompany us?"

"Sure," said the commander. "Colby!" he called out to one of the younger, but no less imposing, team members. "You're with Jordan back to headquarters."

Colby and Jordan began to direct Mac and Emma through the bloody maze when suddenly Emma stopped.

"Wait! The people! There are people in the basement!"

"Yes, ma'am," Jordan said, "we know about them. Your security guard, Peter, has been communicating with the Laurel Police. Everyone is safe. We'll get them all out of here soon."

Colby escorted Emma down the steps as Jordan and Mac followed.

"Mac," Jordan said, his face suddenly serious. "I'm going to be straight with you. You're not in the clear yet."

# Chapter 19

Dwight Holmes had remained across the parking lot when the Laurel Police arrived and the shooting began. He didn't attempt to engage. He knew they were outnumbered, and he knew if Vick didn't survive this situation, he would need to take command. He had mixed feelings about that. Vick had not only been his boss but also his mentor. He felt honored when Vick elevated him to second in command. His pride swelled at the thought of being in command, even though he realized that would mean Vick was dead. He pushed those feelings aside. He needed to assess the situation and decide on how to proceed. He used his cell phone to contact Alexi Russo, the team member who was third in command in their organization, to stand by for orders. He was still on the call when the shooting stopped.

He clicked the button on his team radio, the unspoken signal the team used to request status updates. No one responded, including Vick. He waited a few minutes then signaled again.

"Hold on a minute, Russo." He picked up the binoculars and saw several police officers and several men in what looked like body armor. *Must be NSA*, he thought. His hunch was confirmed when he saw Vernon Jordan exit a vehicle, walk up the steps to what was left of the doors of the bank, and step inside.

"NSA has a team here. I just saw Jordan go in."

"I've told the team to gear up. What do you want us to do?"

"Not sure yet," Holmes replied, holding the phone in one hand and the binoculars in the other. "I need to know Vick's status. If his cover is intact, we may be okay. If not, we have to act. Stand by."

Holmes put the phone on speakerphone and placed it on the van's console. He watched as ambulances began to arrive and collect the dead or wounded. He saw EMTs bringing David Lindsey out on a stretcher. He wasn't in a body bag, so he must be alive but appeared to be unconscious. A few minutes later, he heard an unfamiliar voice on the team radio.

"This is Vernon Jordan. Whoever you are, this is over. Your team is dead. We will find the rest of you."

Holmes heard Russo say "shit." What he didn't hear was Jordan saying anything about Vick. Was he compromised? Was he injured? Dead? If Jordan was aware of Vick's role in this mission, surely he would have said something like, *"oh, and your boss is dead."* But he hadn't said anything about him at all.

Holmes tightened his grip on the binoculars. He had no intention of responding to Jordan's comments. He turned off the radio in the hope it would avoid them tracking his location.

Holmes watched as EMTs emerged from the bank with another stretcher. There was no way to identify who it was because the person was in a body bag. Was it Hollingsworth? A bank employee? Some customer who had been in the wrong place at the wrong time?

His questions were answered when Jordan came out of the bank and handed one of the NSA operatives an evidence bag that contained Vick's team radio. Jordan went back into the bank, and he and another NSA operative escorted a tall, professionally dressed Black woman and MacKenzie Hollingworth.

Holmes threw the binoculars into the passenger seat and picked up his cell phone. "The boss is dead. We need to intercept Jordan before he gets back to NSA. He may have the vials with him. Deploy the team. Now!"

"Where do you want us?"

"Get the team on 29 South before the exit to NSA. If we can't stop them before they take the exit, we won't get them. It's only going to take them about fifteen to twenty minutes to get there from here. What's your ETA?"

"We're close. ETA about ten minutes."

"Move!" Holmes ordered, then started the BGE van to join them.

\* \* \*

NSA agent Colby was driving east on MD 198. The traffic was often heavy in Laurel, but it was only moderately busy today and steadily moving. Colby noticed that a BGE van had passed them on 198 and seemed to be in a hurry, but then slipped directly in front of them as Colby took the 29 North exit. Colby shook his head.

*Some people*, he thought.

Everyone in the car was quiet and the atmosphere tense, so he chose to keep his thoughts to himself.

After merging onto the Parkway, Colby was midway between the exit from 198 and the exit to 32 East, which would take them to NSA, when he noticed the BGE van had stopped on the side of the road up ahead.

"Colby," Jordan said calmly, "use whatever cover you can among the other cars. We're about to be fired upon."

"Sir?"

"Just do it!" Jordan said, then turned to Mac in the back seat. "Mac, there are extra vests in the back. Grab three of them. You and Ms. Bateman put one on and hand the third one to me."

Mac immediately did as he asked. She helped Emma put on hers, handed one to Jordan, then put on one herself.

"Get your heads down," he ordered. "Get on the floor if you can."

No sooner than Jordan finished his instructions, the first shot hit the windshield and narrowly missed Colby, impacting his seat just over his shoulder. Colby and Jordan both knew the NSA vehicle they were in offered more resistance to gunfire than a regular vehicle would, but windows were the weak spots, and the shooter took advantage of that.

Colby weaved into the left lane, putting a Silverado between them and the shooter, but a few moments later, the Silverado veered into the left lane to pass a slower vehicle.

Colby and Jordan were both armed, but Mac's weapon had been taken by the forensics team.

"Hit the van, Colby!" Jordan ordered. "Hit it hard!"

Colby always followed orders. He moved to the right lane, but that put them behind the slower vehicle the Silverado had passed, so he couldn't increase their speed. Colby hoped forty-five miles per hour would be enough. Colby and Jordan both drew their weapons.

"Brace for impact!" Jordan yelled only seconds before Colby turned to hit the side of the van, hoping to flip it over the edge of the shoulder of the road into a ravine.

The front seat airbags deployed on impact, stunning both Colby and Jordan momentarily, but not enough to keep them from shooting the airbags and preparing for their next steps.

Emma and Mac, both in an almost fetal position on the back floorboard, felt like they had been thrown against a brick wall. The episode had happened so quickly that neither of them could process the danger fast enough to scream. After the impact, their bodies hurt, and their brains were just trying to process what had happened.

* * *

Jordan saw that their attack had been successful. The van lay on its side and slid down into the shallow ravine. He didn't see the shooter but hoped he was under the van. He did see a few cars stop on the side of the road, the drivers emerging to try to lend assistance. Jordan couldn't allow that. Not knowing the status of the shooter, he wasn't going to allow civilians to be in harm's way.

"Mac, you and Ms. Bateman stay down. We've got to get these civilians to leave."

"Is the shooter down?" Mac asked, still curled up on the floor.

"Unknown," Jordan responded, "but we'll find out shortly."

"If you don't know and you're leaving us here alone, I need a weapon, Jordan!"

Jordan sighed. She was right. She and the banker would be easy prey if the shooter was alive and able to make it to their vehicle. He pulled his reserve from his ankle and handed it to Mac.

"Are either of you injured?"

"I don't think we know for sure yet. Just go do what you have to do," she said. "We'll manage."

Jordan crept around to the driver's side as Colby was exiting the vehicle. "You take north, and I'll take south. We've got to get the rest of these civilians out of here. Show your creds. I'm calling for backup."

"Yes, sir," Colby said before he moved slowly to the two cars north of them.

Jordan began to move south, aware that if the shooter was still a threat, he was putting himself in the line of fire. As he walked, he called NSA, gave them their location just south of the NSA exit, and requested backup ASAP. The shooter had not fired at him, but he wasn't sure what that meant. He pulled out his credentials and approached the two drivers who had pulled over and were talking together about what they should do.

"Gentlemen, I need you to get back in your cars and continue with your day. Backup is on the way."

One of them eyed Jordan's credentials. "I've already called 911," he said.

Jordan nodded. "Thank you. You did the right thing. I'll deal with them when they arrive. Please be on your way."

The other man looked at Jordan's credentials and then at the weapon he held in his hand. "Is this some kind of national security thing?"

Jordan struggled to be polite but firm. "I'm not at liberty to discuss the situation, sir. I appreciate your interest and willingness to help, but please get in your car and leave the area."

The two men looked at each other, leaving Jordan to wonder if they were going to comply or attack him. Everything suddenly got more complicated when four police cars pulled off the road—two on the north side and the other two across the shallow median on the south side. The officers saw Jordan and Colby's weapons and emerged from their cars with their weapons drawn.

# Chapter 20

Nadia and McKenna stood at the foot of Nadia's bed in the safehouse as she sorted through her go-bag, looking for a shirt for McKenna to wear. She held one up for McKenna and smiled.

"This one is clean, but I did wear it once a few days ago. I'm afraid it's the best I can offer. Do you want to try it?"

McKenna still felt the strange feeling of excitement and anxiety as she stood with Nadia, but simply said, "Sure. I'm sure it will be better than my coffee-soaked shirt." She smiled as she took it from Nadia just as Nadia's phone rang.

Nadia answered the call, then turned to McKenna. "I need to step out and take this call. Besides, you need some privacy to change." She left the room.

McKenna was grateful for a private moment, but she was concerned. The smile had disappeared from Nadia's face as she answered her phone.

McKenna slipped out of her coffee-soaked shirt and used it to dry off what remained of the coffee on her chest and stomach before tossing it on the floor. She slipped Nadia's black T-shirt over her head. She wondered if black was Nadia's signature color or if it was the required color for her job. As the shirt came down over her face, she was once again surprised by a sense of arousal as Nadia's scent entered her nose and seemed to circulate throughout her body.

*This is crazy*, she thought. *Where is this coming from? I don't even really know this woman. I've never felt anything like this before.*

Maybe her body chemistry was off because of the stress or all that had happened. Annie had been killed, she and Mac were in danger, and Nadia helped her feel safe. Yes, that had to be it.

Nadia knocked on the door, and McKenna told her to come in. Nadia's smile had not returned. "I have a couple of updates for you. Maybe we should sit down together." Nadia sat down on the end of the bed and patted it for McKenna to join her. "There was an attack at the local bank where Mac and David Lindsey went together. Mac made it out okay. The man that we believe started all of this was killed. David Lindsey was injured, but Mac was not."

McKenna relaxed for a moment, but Nadia continued.

"There was another altercation as Mac and three others headed to NSA. The situation is still unfolding, but a backup team is close by. Mac and the others are in a vehicle near the NSA exit, so the team should be there in minutes."

McKenna noticed Nadia didn't say that Mac was okay this time, so she struggled to get the question out. "Is Mac okay?"

Nadia touched McKenna on the arm. "She's alive, McKenna, but her condition is unknown right now. They'll let me know when more information is available."

McKenna wasn't sure she could take any more. She began to cry. "She's the only family I have left," was all she could get out between tears.

Nadia squeezed her arm. "I know," she said.

McKenna instinctively put her arms around Nadia. She wasn't concerned about the strange sensations she'd been experiencing. All she felt at the moment was fear for her sister and reached out for comfort from the only other person present.

McKenna had stopped crying and pulled away. "I'm so sorry," she said. "I didn't mean to do that."

"No apologies necessary, McKenna. When people are going through a tough time like you are now, sometimes they need a little comfort."

McKenna nodded. "Thanks for understanding—and for the shirt. It fits just fine."

"I'm glad," Nadia's smile was back. "Sometimes during difficult times, it helps to do something ordinary. Why don't you take your shirt to the laundry room and see if you can find something in there to help you get rid of those stains."

They both got up and went toward the kitchen. Nadia stopped there to talk with Martinez, and McKenna continued to the utility room.

Martinez gave Nadia a crooked smile that signaled an unspoken comment.

"Don't start with me, Martinez," she said firmly. "We're on a case right now, and that's it."

Martinez raised both hands in a gesture of surrender.

McKenna sorted through the various laundry supplies but wasn't sure there was anything that would remove coffee stains from her pink plaid flannel shirt. She finally settled on a combination of stain removers, which she applied to the stains, and then tossed it into the washing machine with regular detergent. Her eyes were a little swollen from her most recent crying spell, so she struggled to read the controls on the machine. It seemed silly to wash one shirt, but Nadia was right. It seemed to help a little to do something normal.

*Nadia*, she thought. *How can I allow myself to be so distracted by her when Mac is in danger?*

She didn't have an answer for herself, but she remembered a moment when she had her arms around Nadia and was crying. Between the moment when her tears stopped and she finally pulled away, she remembered the smell of Nadia's hair against her face. She pulled up the top of Nadia's T-shirt that she was now wearing and found the same scent. She breathed it in and then let the shirt go back to its normal position. She felt a lighter version of the attraction she had felt before, but this time, the most noticeable feelings were comfort and safety.

# Chapter 21

"Put your weapons down slowly, kick them away from you, and put your hands up!" one officer on each side of the road ordered.

Jorden and Colby did exactly as ordered. The civilian drivers with them instinctively raised their hands.

One officer from each group approached Colby and another approached Jordan as the others kept their weapons trained on them. Colby and Jordan both still had their credentials in their hands from showing them to the civilians present.

The officer who approached Jordan saw the black leather item in his hand and said, "Toss whatever you're holding over to me."

Jordan complied.

There were several weapons aimed at Jordan, but this officer was not taking any chances. "Cover me!" he yelled to his nearby colleagues before reaching down to pick up the wallet. "NSA, huh?" he asked.

"Yes, Officer, I am. So is the other armed man up there." Jordan motioned toward Colby with his head.

"I'm going to have to verify this," the officer said, waving Jordan's credential wallet.

"You should be able to do that in a few minutes. We have a backup team due here any minute."

"Yeah," the officer said, "with the same IDs, I suppose."

"Yes," Jordan sighed, "with the same IDs. Go ahead and check us out, Officer, but please hurry. There's an active shooter beneath or beside that BGE van over there." Jordan motioned again with his head.

"What's going on here, Mr..." he looked at the ID again, "Agent Jordan?"

Jordan pursed his lips. "I know this is going to sound like a cliché to you, Officer, but I can't explain this situation to you. It's a matter of national security. There are also two women in the backseat of our vehicle who may be injured and may be unable to safely get out."

"National security," the officer said as he tapped Jordan's credential wallet against the side of his leg. His thoughts about what to do next were interrupted when a rifle shot came from somewhere near the BGE van.

All the officers on the scene took cover but kept their weapons on Colby and Jordan, who both suddenly hit the ground, along with the civilian drivers. But the shot wasn't fired in their direction; it had been fired toward the SUV. A shot from a handgun returned fire from the SUV.

"Officer, the shooter is aiming at the SUV. One of the women is armed and has returned fire, but she needs help!"

Holmes' rifle shot had shattered the window of the backseat of the NSA vehicle on Mac's side.

*Where in the hell is my team?* he thought.

* * *

Mac shifted a little to test the status of her injuries. Several body parts were in pain, but the worst seemed to be on her right side. She struggled to pull herself up by pushing on the floorboard and then on the seat enough to reach the shattered window and return fire.

Emma was silent. Mac didn't know if she was dead, unconscious, or too terrified to speak, but she was on the opposite side of the car, and Mac's body was between her and the shooter.

Mac felt a sudden, searing pain in the calf of her right leg and decided she must have been shot. She had to get herself in a better defensive position. She had no idea when help was coming, and she and Emma were on their own. Mac was the only one with a weapon, though, so she had to protect them both. She slowly and painfully rolled over on the floorboard so that she was lying on her back facing the broken window. She had never felt the kind of pain she felt in her right side and right leg, and she decided that she probably had a few broken ribs in addition to being shot.

"Emma," she whispered. "Emma, are you okay?" When Emma didn't respond, Mac tilted her head back and used it to nudge Emma. "Emma, are you okay?"

Emma finally groaned and responded, "I think so. I haven't tried to move yet, though."

"Well don't try," Mac whispered. "I think you're in the safest position you can be in right now."

With Emma curled up on the floor, the Kevlar vest was covering the most exposed part of her body.

Mac's attention was drawn to what sounded like movement near their vehicle. She painfully raised her weapon and aimed it at the broken window using both hands, which she suddenly noticed were shaking. She also heard a lot of shouting from the surrounding area, but there were too many voices overlapping each other to make out what anyone was saying. What she did know was that no one had come to help them, and that wasn't a good sign.

*Where is everybody*, she wondered, keeping her eyes trained on the missing window.

* * *

Outside, Holmes moved his head just enough to see several black SUVs moving toward the scene. NSA, he thought. *Once they sort the situation out with the police, it's all over. It's now or never.*

He had been slowly crawling toward the SUV, making as little noise as possible. He suspected that the NSA vehicle was armored, which meant he would have to stand up to take his shot at Hollingsworth.

*So be it*, he thought. *There's no way out of this now.*

Holmes was keenly aware of the presence of the many other weapons that were probably aimed in his direction, but he was determined to kill Hollingsworth. She had been a thorn in Vick's side throughout this mission, and he knew Vick intended to kill her. Since Vick had not survived the situation at the bank and Hollingsworth *had* somehow survived, he concluded she must have been responsible for his death. That was hard to believe. She was a just Navy musician, and Vick was a trained professional in a more lethal field, but somehow things had worked out that way. That was unacceptable. It was his job to finish the mission—at least this part of it. In his current situation, killing her might be the last thing he would be able to do, but he was determined to do it. He spotted an opening in the wreckage by the back passenger door and took another shot

Just after doing so, he saw the black SUVs pull up on both sides of the parkway. His instincts and experience told him these were NSA agents, and he began to run scenarios in his head about how this encounter might play out. None of them were good.

NSA agents took charge of the scene and covered the area in his direction. They had twelve agents on site. There was nowhere for him to go except into the woods on foot, and success was unlikely. There was no way for Holmes to get away. He watched as the police officers cleared out the civilian drivers, and closed off parkway traffic in both directions.

The senior office raised a megaphone. "Shooter, you have no way out. Put your weapon down and come out with your hands above your head!"

Holmes did not respond. He knew it was time. He was only thirty-five years old and hadn't planned to die on this mission, but that was the hand he'd been dealt. He believed in the mission. He had been one of the first people Vick had recruited. Vick convinced him the United States government was not taking North Korea seriously enough. He said they were a 'clear and present danger' that needed to be eliminated to save American lives. That was ten years ago.

He—and others that Vick recruited—considered themselves at war with North Korea. He knew Vick had explained that to Hollingsworth, but she still got in their way. Soldiers die in war. Maybe it was his time. It was her time, too.

He knew he probably had one shot before he would be fired upon, so he readied himself. His left leg hurt. It might even be broken, but he pushed himself up from the ground and balanced on his right leg to stand up. He aimed his rifle through the broken window and was surprised to find Hollingsworth staring up at him with her weapon ready. Mac fired without hesitation. Holmes was hit in the chest and slumped to the ground.

"Shooter's down!" she yelled. "Get us out of here!"

Holmes was still holding his weapon as he lay on the ground. He told himself to raise it, but his body was unable to comply. As he slipped into unconsciousness, the last thing he saw was a group of NSA agents in tactical gear approaching him with caution. One of them reached him and removed his rifle.

"He's wearing a vest. He's alive, just knocked out. Get him out of here but cuff him."

Two EMTs loaded Holmes into an ambulance, his hands each cuffed to the rails of the stretcher.

"Take him to Fort Meade," Jordan ordered.

The EMTs looked at each other, but one of the other NSA agents felt the need to clarify the order. "Do as he says."

"Jordan," Mac yelled, "is that you?"

"Yeah, it's me, Mac—and a bunch of other people."

"Get us out of here!"

"We're about to do that, Mac. I need you to toss your weapon out the window first."

"After all of this, you don't trust me?"

"I do trust you, Mac," he said calmly, "but we've got to do this by the book."

Mac did as he directed. "Now please get Emma out first. She hasn't moved and doesn't know if she's injured."

"Are you injured?"

"Yeah," Mac answered. "I think I have some broken ribs, and that guy shot me in the leg."

"We've got enough people here to get you both out."

# Chapter 22

Russo and the rest of Vick's backup team found themselves delayed by traffic on MD 32 East, which had suddenly seemed to stop.

*Damn*, he thought, *there must be a wreck up ahead.*

He asked the guy in the passenger seat, Marks, to find an alternate route. The search didn't take long.

Marks said, "Take the next exit for Route 1 South. We can work our way around from there."

*I hope so*, thought Russo. *Holmes is counting on us.*

He had told Holmes they were ten minutes away, but that ETA was no longer true. He tried to reach Holmes on the radio by clicking the team's signal, but there was no response. That could mean he had turned his radio off for some reason or was otherwise unable or unwilling to respond. Russo didn't like any of those possibilities. He continued to move toward the Route 1 exit at the snail's pace the traffic allowed. He had considered driving down the shoulder but didn't know the area or the road well enough to determine if that was possible. He also didn't want to attract attention. He had noticed several police cars and other emergency vehicles making their way through the traffic. This pace would have to do—for now.

They reached the exit for Route 1 and headed south toward Laurel. They were lucky enough with the timing of traffic lights that they made better time on Route 1, but as they exited onto 198, traffic was heavy in the eastbound lane. Traffic in the westbound lane was sparse and moved at a steady pace. Police were posted along the way, stopping drivers, and giving instructions. Russo, Marks, and the others hid their weapons under their seats as one of the officers approached their vehicle.

"What's the problem, Officer?" Russo asked in his most polite voice.

"There's a problem on the Parkway. That's why all this traffic is backed up. Where are you folks heading? I noticed your camo. You guys been hunting?"

Russo's mind raced for a plausible reply. "Nah, we were planning to, but some family stuff came up. We're headed back home."

"Where are your weapons?" the officer asked, trying to see toward the back of the SUV.

"In the back," Russo replied, suddenly nervous that the officer might want to see them and their firearms licenses. "You want to see our licenses?" he finally asked, reaching for his wallet.

The officer waved him off. "No, you guys seem okay to me. We need to get this traffic cleared out. Which way are you headed?"

Russo was relieved there would be no confrontation with the officer. They didn't need things to get any worse, but his temper was holding by a thread. He ran his hand through his dark hair. "We live in different directions. You got any suggestions?"

"Well, if you need to go south, I suggest you take 197. The Parkway is accessible there. If you need to go north, I suggest you turn around at the next intersection and go up Route 1."

"Thank you, Officer, you've been very helpful." He turned to Marks. "Watch for 197. We've got to stop somewhere long enough to contact the others and figure out what to do." He banged his hand on the steering wheel.

*We've got to get out of here! This wasn't the Capitol Beltway; it was Laurel, Maryland. We can't be that far from Holmes!*

Marks alerted him to the turn-off to 197. They traveled among others who had been rerouted in this direction, but traffic seemed to be moving well. A couple of miles up the road was a shopping complex with fast food restaurants and lots of parking. Russo pulled into the complex and found several parking places in the back of the parking lot near some tall trees.

"What's up, boss?" Marks asked, confused.

"I've got to make a phone call or two. Holmes is out there on his own, and we can't get to him. I don't even know who's in command right now." He got out of the vehicle and dialed a number he had memorized years ago but had never dialed.

A woman's voice answered. "Sitrep, Russo," she said.

Russo was surprised she knew his name. He didn't know hers. He didn't even know it would be a woman who answered. This was a number he hoped he never had to call. It was a number of last resort, to be used only when a mission had been compromised with no hope of completion.

"Agma is dead. I don't know Holmes' status. I am unable to reach him. Our team was en route to him when traffic was suddenly rerouted. I need command instructions."

"Hold," was the woman's curt response, but the hold didn't last long. "Remain in current location for one hour then return to quarters. Prepare for a secure video meeting this evening, 6 P.M." She ended the call.

Russo stared at his phone as if he had never seen it before. He wasn't sure what he expected, but this wasn't it. He stood still for a moment, trying to get a grip on the situation. He had been given strange orders, but he had been trained to follow orders. It was up to him that the rest of his team do the same.

When he got back into the vehicle, the eyes of the other five team members were all on him. No one spoke. "We've got new orders," he said, with as much confidence as his voice would allow. "We're to remain here for one hour then return to quarters and prepare for a video conference at six."

There was silence for several seconds before Marks asked the question on everyone's mind. "What about Holmes, boss? He's out there alone."

Russo looked him directly in the eyes and repeated what he had told the woman. "Agma is dead. I don't know Holmes' status. I am unable to reach him. I am to assume command until further notice."

That's not exactly what the woman had told him, but everyone knew he was next in the line of command behind Holmes.

"We've got an hour to kill," he said. "There are a bunch of food places here. Let's get something to eat so we'll be ready for the video conference."

The others took turns looking at each other for some clue as to how to respond. They were all former members of one branch or another of the military, but they all believed in the same creed: 'No man left behind.'

# Chapter 23

Holmes woke up with a start. He was in a hospital room, and each of his hands was cuffed to the bedrail. The vest had saved his life, but the proximity of the shot and his broken leg had caused him to fall and hit his head on a wayward chunk of concrete along the roadside. He was surprised to be alive. Surprised, but not entirely sure he was glad. He was in custody and would, more than likely, spend the rest of his days in prison. Death might have been a better outcome. There were no magic 'deals' for guys like him. An armed police officer stood next to the door of his hospital room.

He didn't speak to the guard, and the guard didn't speak to him. As he contemplated the events that brought him here, the door opened. Vernon Jordan walked in and took a chair by the side of the hospital bed.

"Mr. Holmes." Jordan began. "You've been a busy man. I don't suppose you want to tell me what you've been up to today."

"I want a lawyer," was all Holmes said.

"Yeah," Jordan said with a slight smile. "I thought you might say something like that. The thing is, you know, some of your activity seems to fall into the category of domestic terrorism. That complicates things a bit, don't you think?"

"Get the hell out of here." Holmes attempted to spit in Jordan's direction, but it got no farther than his own arm.

Jordan lost his slight smile. "Have it your way, Mr. Holmes."

* * *

At the end of the same hall, Mac woke up to find herself also cuffed to the bed rail and under armed guard. It hurt to breathe, and her body seemed to hurt all over, like she'd been in a car wreck. *Oh, yeah, I was.* She noticed the calf of her right leg had been bandaged.

There was a knock on the door, and the guard put his hand on his weapon.

Jordan held up his credentials. "Vernon Jordan, NSA, officer. I'd like to speak with Ms. Hollingsworth."

The guard relaxed his stance and allowed Jordan to enter.

Jordan took a seat next to the hospital bed. He glanced at the officer. "You may remove the cuffs from Ms. Hollingsworth." The officer hesitated but only momentarily. He had been ordered to cooperate with Vernon Jordan. "Verify with whoever you need to, officer."

"No need, sir. I have orders to cooperate with you and follow your instructions."

"Thank you." He turned to Mac, who was now rubbing her wrists that had been chaffed by the cuffs. "My God, Mac."

"My God, what, Vernon? I didn't have anything to do with any of this, but suddenly I'm not trusted anymore?"

"No, I'm sorry about that turn of events. It wasn't my doing. Sullivan and the rest just thought there were some unexplained coincidences and more of a connection with you and David than there was. Most of that has been cleared up now. It took some doing, but you're not implicated in this case in any way."

"What do you mean? What *hasn't* been cleared up?"

"Maybe we should wait until you're feeling better. Besides, there are some things going on that I hope will clear things up completely."

"Please don't leave me hanging like that, Vernon. Tell me what's wrong."

Jordan seemed uncomfortable. "Maybe you should have an attorney present."

"What?" Mac's whole body jerked, which caused her pain to spike. "I don't need an attorney Jordan. I haven't done anything wrong! We've known each other a long time, Vernon. Don't *you* even trust me?"

Jordan rubbed his eyes and ran his fingers through his hair. "Mac, did David Lindsey give you an envelope when you were with him?"

Mac frowned. "Yeah, he did. He had written on the front of the envelope *Read Later*. When I asked him about it, all he would say was 'just read it later.' Why?"

"Did you ever read it?

"Are you kidding me? With everything that's been going on since I met him at my apartment, I haven't even thought about it! Why are you asking me about it? Why don't you ask David about it?"

Jordan took a deep breath. "David Lindsey died in surgery, Mac. The envelope was found on you when they brought you here. It was taken with your other things in evidence bags to NSA." He took another deep breath. "We opened it, Mac. There was a name, a phone number, and a very short note. That's all I'm at liberty to tell you. NSA is working on that now. I'm sure when they've figured out what it means, everything will be fine."

Mac frowned and looked away. "Is this ever going to be over, Vernon? I want my life back." She offered a wry smile. "I know this probably sounds crazy to you, but I haven't touched my horn in days." She knew it was unlikely that a non-musician would understand the importance of that.

Jordan chuckled. "Wow. After all you've been through, you're thinking about how long it's been since you've played your horn?" He shook his head. "I know you want your life back, Mac. I'm working on it, as are others." His look turned sympathetic. "Can I get you anything? Anything except your horn?"

Mac smiled and thought for a moment. "Yeah, two things, I think. I'd love to have a good cup of coffee—not hospital coffee, good coffee, light roast, black."

Jordan smiled. "And the other thing?"

"I'd really like to see my sister. Can I do that, Vernon? I'd like to know she's okay, and I'd like for her to know that I'm okay."

Jordan motioned toward her leg and the bruises that were showing on every visible body part. "You're not exactly what I'd call okay," he said.

"No, maybe not okay, but I am alive. Can you make that happen?"

He nodded. "I think I can make that happen."

* * *

Jordan walked a few doors down from Mac's hospital room and knocked.

Emma Bateman said, "Come in."

He entered to find her propped up in her hospital bed. An older, Black couple sat beside her bed.

"Mom and Dad," she said, extending her hand to shake Jordan's hand, "this is Agent Jordan. Agent Jordan, these are my parents, Marian Bateman and Dr. William Bateman."

Both the man and the woman rose to shake Jordan's hand.

"Ms. Bateman," Jordan said after the introductions were complete, "do you feel up to talking about what happened at the bank this morning?"

"Yes," Emma said with a nod, "what would you like to know?"

Dr. Bateman interrupted to ask, "Agent Jordan, does Emma need to have an attorney present before she answers your questions?"

Jordan shook his head. "No, sir. We know Emma shot Captain Vick, but bank cameras and his own voice recordings that we've reviewed make it clear he was not who he appeared to be. He was, in fact, a very dangerous man." He looked at Emma. "Your daughter acted very bravely, saving the life of MacKenzie Hollingsworth and probably her own life as well. She will not be prosecuted for her actions."

Emma told him David had been a special customer for her for several years, and, although she didn't really consider them to be friends, he was friendly to her. She said that when David came in that morning so early with Mac, she thought it was to introduce him to her and thought they might be a couple. She said she felt honored he would do so. Then she described how David had used the dry-erase board to warn her of the coming danger and asked her to get everyone to a safe place.

Emma's hands were together in her lap, and she looked down at them. Jordan suspected this gentle woman was struggling with the fact that she had picked up a gun and killed a man. He knew the emotional weight that came with ending someone's life. He had felt it many times.

"Emma? Are you okay?" her mother asked.

Emma looked back at her mother and nodded. "Yes. It's hard knowing I killed a man, but it helps to know I saved the lives of others. I couldn't do that as a child, but I did it this morning."

Jordan was confused by her response. "I don't understand," he said.

Emma's father started to explain to protect Emma from having to discuss what she experienced in Rwanda, but Emma held up her hand.

"It's okay, Dad. I can tell him." Emma looked at Jordan and told him about hiding in the big tree as a child and seeing her family and friends murdered in the Rwandan genocide. "I couldn't do anything to help them. I had no weapons. I was a child, and I was so very afraid." Tears ran down her cheeks. "This morning, I was still afraid, but I thought I could do something that would protect other people—and protect myself. When I saw the gun on the floor, I felt like I was moving in slow motion when I picked it up. So much was going on, that man didn't seem to be paying any attention to me. Somehow the fear passed, and I suddenly felt strong—and I aimed and fired." She looked at Jordan. "I've never fired a weapon before. I've never even touched one."

Jordan was deeply touched by her story of both experiences. He sat down in a chair opposite her parents. He placed his hand gently on top of hers and said softly, "Thank you, Emma, for telling me about both of those experiences. You couldn't save your family and friends in Rwanda, but you did save lives today, including your own."

"What about David Lindsey?" she asked. "Is he okay?"

Jordan looked at Emma's parents, who both had tears in their eyes, and then back at Emma. "I'm sorry, Emma. David Lindsey died in surgery a short time ago."

Emma simply nodded her understanding, but her tears continued. Finally, she managed another question. "Why did that man want to kill David and Ms. Hollingsworth? He wanted something from them. What was it?"

Jordan struggled with his response. He knew from the information from the other bank employees that David was a special customer to Emma for some reason. The answers she sought involved classified information he couldn't disclose, and despite David's role in all of this, he saw no reason to tarnish Emma's memory of him. He settled for what he hoped would be an acceptable answer.

"David and Ms. Hollingsworth were both veterans. They were both doing their best to protect our country from a very dangerous man—and you helped them do that, Emma." He paused for a moment, hoping Emma wouldn't ask any more questions. He decided to preempt her and her parents from doing so by adding, "I'm afraid that's all I'm at liberty to share with you."

Jordan was relieved Emma and her parents seemed satisfied with his answer.

"So what about you, Emma?" he said in a lighter tone of voice, "When will you be able to go home?"

Emma's response was also lighter. "This afternoon, I think. My leg was injured in the crash, but it wasn't broken. They tell me it should be better in a couple of weeks. Other than that, just some bruises and soreness. I was very lucky. How is Ms. Hollingsworth?

"She was shot in the leg and, like you, has a lot of bruises and soreness from the crash, but she's going to be okay."

Emma smiled for the first time since Jordan had entered the room. "I'm glad to hear that. David seemed to really care about her."

Jordan wasn't sure if that was true or not but decided not to address it. "I think it's time for me to leave you good people alone so Emma can get on with getting ready to leave."

There were handshakes all around once again, then Jordan left the room.

# Chapter 24

Russo, Marks, and the rest of their team divided their fast food attention between Taco Bell and McDonald's and rejoined each other in the vehicle to eat and wait until the designated time for them to return to quarters. They were all big men with big appetites, but they ate their food in silence. Each one of them wondered what had happened to Holmes, but when their new orders didn't include any mention of him, they all assumed the worst.

"Do you think he's dead, Russo?" Marks finally asked.

Russo stopped chewing his burrito and took a long sip of his Coke to wash it down. "I don't know, Marks. We never leave a guy behind. We've all always agreed to that. Vick agreed to that. The folks giving the orders now? I don't really know them, but I think Vick handpicked all of us." He took another big bite of his burrito, chewed it slowly, and swallowed. "He's got to be dead, Marks. I think they would have sent us after him otherwise."

Marks looked first at Russo and then at Richards and Torro in the back seat. They were looking at each other and gave a slight shake of their heads. They continued to eat and drink and wait in silence.

Russo kept glancing at the clock on the vehicle's console. He'd had to wait for action many times in the Army, but those were times waiting to attack, not retreat, and even though he'd told Marks he thought Holmes was dead, he felt like they had been ordered to retreat. He didn't like that.

"It's time," he finally said. "Let's get out of here."

He pulled out of the parking lot and headed toward MD 197. As they passed the exit for 295 South, they saw that the police officer had been correct about being able to access the Parkway at that point. There was a long time of traffic to take the exit, but they didn't need to go that way. They remained on 197 heading toward MD 301, which would take them to a secluded farm near Edgewater, Maryland.

They were still twenty minutes from the farm when Russo's 'last resort' phone rang.

"Russo."

"There's been a change in plans. When you arrive at quarters, pack up all the gear and wipe the place down. A truck will pick up the equipment at midnight, and a silent chopper will pick up your team."

"Where are we going?"

"You'll find out when you get there."

"What about Holmes?" he asked with an edge to his voice.

There was a brief pause from the other person on the line before the woman said, "Holmes didn't make it. He's dead. The rest of you are being reassigned." She then ended the call.

Russo put the phone back in his pocket and struggled to sort out the change in plans and the news of Holmes' death. He didn't think the injuries Holmes sustained in the attack had been that serious. Maybe he had a heart attack or something. That seemed unlikely, though. Holmes was in top physical condition and was only thirty years old. Something must have happened at the hospital. Maybe he tried to escape and was shot. Russo was frustrated that the woman had ended the call without giving him a chance to ask questions. He could call her back, of course, but something told him that wasn't a good idea. Those folks didn't like to be questioned.

"What is it, man?" Marks asked, nudging Russo from his thoughts.

"Holmes is dead. We're all being reassigned."

"No way, man! What happened?"

"Look, she hung up before I could ask anything. I'm not calling her back. Do you want to call her, Marks?" Russo knew the answer before Marks responded.

Marks settled back into his seat, and Russo saw in the rear-view mirror that the others had grown quiet and were doing the same.

"No, man, I don't want to do that."

"I didn't think so," Russo responded. "Let's just get to the farm. They want us to pack things up and wipe it all down. A truck will pick up the equipment at midnight, and they're sending a silent chopper to pick us up."

"Where are we going?" Diaz, one of the guys in the back, asked.

"I don't know." Russo struggled to be steady in his tone, but the uncertainty was evident.

There was no further conversation as they continued toward the farm. When they arrived, Russo divided the team in half—one half to pack up all the gear and the other half to clear the house of any evidence of their time there. He put Marks in charge of the gear-packing team, and he directed those working in the house.

"I don't want anything left behind," he told them. "Not a fingerprint, hair, food, trash—nothing. Richards, you gather the electronics—all of them."

Russo felt uneasy about these new orders. Nothing they had been ordered to do was part of any contingency plan that had been discussed as they prepared for this mission. Maybe it was Vick's unexpected death that had thrown things off. The head of their organization, the man who had conceived all of their plans, was gone. Russo was angry with Vick about putting himself in harm's way. He was also angry about Holmes' death. He knew Vick had been shot, but the information they had been given indicated that Holmes' injuries had not been serious.

He pondered these thoughts as he worked with the team to clear the house. He knew the men on his team wondered about Holmes, too. His 'last resort' phone rang.

"Russo," he said.

The woman on the other end said, "ETA of the truck and chopper is thirty minutes. Your team needs to be ready when they arrive."

"Understood," Russo said, "we're just finishing up things now." He knew the woman often ended their calls once she was satisfied the conversation had ended. Most of the time he was satisfied, too, but not this time. "Ma'am?" he said quickly, hoping to keep her on the line for a question they all had. "The team wants to know about Holmes, ma'am. How did he die?"

There was a brief pause from the woman on the other end of the call before she responded, "He died in the line of duty."

# Chapter 25

The police officer stationed at Holmes' hospital room opened the door. "Your lawyer is here to see you," he said as he ushered in a woman who was professionally dressed but looked too young to be out of law school.

Holmes clicked off the TV, which was the only thing within his reach with the handcuffs on.

"A *woman*?" he said. "And not just a woman, a young woman." In his head, he added *a young Black woman* but decided to keep that to himself. He shook his head and then asked, "Are you really a lawyer?"

"I am," she said. "And I drew the short straw for your case, Mr. Holmes. If you would prefer a different attorney, I will convey your request to the judge, but you might be even less pleased with the next choice." She sat down beside his bed. "You've been charged with some very serious crimes, Mr. Holmes, and they carry serious penalties. Now shall we get on with this, or would you like for me to leave?"

Holmes shook his hands in anger, rattling the handcuffs attached to his hospital bed and dropping his TV remote. He cursed under his breath, then let out a big sigh. "Fine," he said. "What can you do for me?"

"In all honesty, probably not much. You've been charged with illegal possession of a firearm, attempted murder, firing at a federal agent, and conspiracy to commit an act of terrorism. What is it that you think I could do for you?"

"Get me out of here," he said softly. "I hate hospitals."

Toni nodded and made a few notes on the tablet she had taken from her briefcase. "I will check with your doctor and see if your condition will allow you to be transferred to a secure location at Fort Meade." She finished writing her notes, then added, "I don't think you'll find your new location any more comfortable, though."

"So they'll put me in a cell. Fine! At least I can get rid of these!" he rattled the handcuffs again.

"Okay," she said. "Let me see what I can do about that. In the meantime, don't answer any questions unless I'm with you. Understood?"

"Yeah, I get it," he replied without looking at her.

He didn't understand. It sounded like this woman was a public defender. Where was the legal counsel he was supposed to get from the Agma organization? That was always the way it worked. When any of them ran into trouble with the law, Vick had sent in an attorney who was part of the organization. He knew Vick was gone, but those operational procedures were designed to cover them.

*They've cut me off*, he thought with a sudden wave of fear. *Why would they do that?*

As he pondered that question, the guard opened his door again. A young man in a white coat came in with a multi-section plastic tote that held a variety of supplies for lab tests.

"They just did this yesterday," Holmes protested. He was tired of being restrained, tired of the IV in his arm, and tired of people poking him with needles. He was a fearless soldier in battle, but the indignities he suffered here were almost too much for him.

"Your doctor is thinking of discharging you and wants a current set of labs," the young man explained as the guard left him to his duties.

But the young man didn't draw his blood. He gave Holmes an injection. Just as Holmes started to ask what it was, he noticed a strange sensation moving through his body. By the time he tried to open his mouth to speak, he found that he couldn't. In fact, he couldn't move at all. He could see the young man standing over him, but he couldn't move any part of his body.

"You have served Agma with honor. We cannot, however, run the risk of you disclosing any information about the organization or its plans—regardless of whether the information is disclosed willingly or unwillingly. We're sure you understand."

Holmes continued to watch with horror as the young man injected him with a second liquid, then turned and left the room. He stopped to tell the guard at the door that Holmes asked not to be disturbed for a while because he wanted to get some sleep.

The police officer smiled. "Well, you know how hard it can be to get any sleep in a hospital—especially in handcuffs, right?"

The young man smiled back and gave the officer a fist bump. "Yeah, you know it."

* * *

Only a few minutes later, Toni Williams returned to Holmes' hospital room. The guard at the door told her the lab technician had just left and said that Holmes didn't want to be disturbed so he could get some sleep.

Toni rolled her eyes. "Well, I just talked with his doctor, and they're going to discharge him today. I'm sure he won't mind being disturbed by that news."

The guard shrugged, and Toni pushed open the door.

"Mr. Holmes, I have some good news," she began.

She noticed that Holmes didn't respond at all—no words, no movement, not even a look in her direction. She walked to the side of his hospital bed and saw his eyes fixed in a vacant stare. He wasn't breathing. She rushed out the door and called for help. Holmes' doctor was still nearby on a computer. He and two nurses ran to the room. One of the nurses called a code for a crash cart so they could restart his heart if that was the problem, but after the doctor examined Holmes, he canceled the code.

"He's gone. What the hell happened?" he asked no one in particular before noticing needle pricks on Holmes' arm. "Someone gave him an injection, maybe two. I didn't order any injections for this patient."

The doctor stared down at Holmes. The nurses began moving to remove Holmes' IV but stopped as the doctor raised a hand to halt them.

"No. Don't anyone touch anything," he ordered, surprising the nurses who had gathered to assist. He turned to one of the nurses and said, "Call the police. I think our patient might have been murdered."

\* \* \*

Jordan left Emma's room and stepped into the stairwell to call Nadia. She answered on the second ring. "Hey, it's Jordan," he said. "How are things going there?"

"All quiet here. We haven't had any problems." She paused a moment. "Anything happening that we should know about on your end?"

Jordan chuckled to himself. "Yeah, a lot, actually, but we'll catch up later." He sat down on one of the steps. "I need you and Martinez to bring McKenna to the hospital. Mac asked to see her, and I don't see a problem with that right now, except..."

"Sir?"

"We don't know how many more of Agma's people are out there. Just take extra precautions."

"Understood, sir. I think McKenna will be glad to get out of here for a while."

"Oh, and one more thing," he said. "Please pick up a cup of light roast coffee, black. It's the only other thing Mac asked for."

Nadia laughed. "Of course, sir. I will keep you informed."

They ended the call, and Jordan exited the stairwell to continue down the hall toward the elevators. Many things were happening at NSA that he wanted to be involved with, but he also knew that wasn't going to happen. He was, however, anxious to learn what progress had been made, especially where Mac was concerned.

He saw several police officers, led by a man and a woman in plain clothes, moving in the direction of Holmes' room. Jordan walked up to them and showed them his credentials.

"What's up?" he asked.

Both of them barely glanced at Jordan's credentials, but also flashed theirs. He noted their names: Detectives Solomon and Barnes.

"Your prisoner is dead, Mr. Jordan."

"What?" Jordan was aghast. "When? How?"

"Short while ago, it seems." Solomon gestured with his head toward Holmes' doctor. "The doc here thinks your prisoner may have been murdered."

Detective Barnes added, "This is a suspected homicide at a civilian hospital, Mr. Jordan, but we've been ordered—by the White House, in fact—to assist NSA. How do you want this to go?"

Shocked, Jordan held up a finger and said, "Give me a minute, Detectives." He stepped back into the stairwell and dialed General Sullivan's office. "Amber, this is Jordan. I need to speak with the General or Deputy Director Clement right away."

There was a brief pause, then Amber said, "I have both of them on the line, sir."

Jordan explained that Holmes was dead and two homicide detectives had arrived on the scene. After some discussion, Sullivan made a decision.

"Let them investigate, Vernon. They'll do a fine job. We've got a lot going on here right now. Stay on it and keep us updated."

"Yes, sir." He was hoping to learn that Mac was finally in the clear, so he added, "General, is there any update you can give me on the work there?"

"Not at this time, but you will be informed when there is."

"Thank you, sir."

There was a pause on the NSA side of the conversation, then Sullivan added, "We were just about to video conference with the president. We have the vials, and we hoped the threat was contained. If one of Agma's men has been murdered, though, it makes me doubt this thing is over."

"Yes, sir," Jordan responded. "I've wondered the same thing myself, sir."

The call ended. Jordan called Nadia again.

"What's your ETA?"

"Depending on traffic, fifteen to twenty minutes." She paused. "Problem, sir?"

"Yeah, could be. Holmes is dead. Homicide detectives are here. Just stay sharp." He ended the call without sharing any additional information, then exited the stairwell again to talk with Detective Solomon. "Your investigation," he said, "just keep me in the loop."

"Understood," Solomon curtly replied.

"There is something else I need, though, Det. Solomon." He motioned toward the other end of the hall where Mac and Emma's rooms were located. "I need additional security on two other patients here. I want one guard outside the room and one guard inside the room." Solomon and Barnes both nodded, then Jordan added, "I would also like to be present when the officer guarding this prisoner is questioned."

"No problem," Solomon responded with a raised eyebrow that suggested to Jordan that he might, indeed, have a problem with that.

Jordan headed for the vending machines near the elevators. One of them was a coffee machine, and Jordan reluctantly swiped his card and made his selection—dark and black. He waited as the cup filled up and then took a tentative sip. The coffee wasn't hot, and it tasted like something that had been brewing all day. He cursed and tossed it into the trash.

"You're right, Mac," he said to himself. He remembered there was a kiosk near the hospital entrance called Best Brew, so he took the elevator down to get a cup there. *I may as well get one for Mac, too*, he thought.

As he exited the elevator on the ground floor and headed for the kiosk, he called Nadia back and told her to skip stopping for Mac's coffee and to get there as soon as possible.

"Has there been a development?" she asked.

"Yes, and I'll brief you when you get here."

* * *

Nadia was about to ask another question, but she was good at reading the tone of someone's voice. His tone had been stressed. She felt the hair on the back of her neck prick up—a well-developed indicator of danger.

"McKenna," she turned to address Mac's sister in the back seat. "Reach into the back of the SUV and grab a Kevlar vest and helmet."

"What?" McKenna was horrified. "What's wrong?"

Nadia shook her head. "Maybe nothing," she said, "but I've been doing this for a while, and I trust my instincts. Just do it. Put them on and then get as low as possible on the floor. Don't get back up again until I tell you to." McKenna seemed unable or unwilling to move. "Kenna!" she yelled, "do it now!"

McKenna finally emerged from her frozen state and complied.

Martinez was driving and listened to this exchange with interest. "What's up, Tosh?"

"I'm not sure," she said quietly. "I've just got a bad feeling about this."

# Chapter 26

Elliott Hirsch, the young man who killed Holmes, stepped off the elevator on the ground floor of the hospital and saw a man and a woman in plain clothes followed by four police officers enter through the front entrance. He quickly turned down the hall to his right where he knew there might be another way out for him. He found a men's bathroom, entered, and locked the door. He removed the top of the large waste can and dumped half of its contents on the floor. He pulled off his lab coat and scrubs and wrapped the tote full of lab testing equipment in them, shoved them into the waste can, and quickly gathered the trash on the floor to add back on top of them.

*I'm glad I'm wearing gloves*, he thought. *This stuff is nasty.*

He had prepared for his escape by putting on street clothes under his scrubs. Three layers of clothing had been uncomfortable for a while, but more comfortable than getting caught. Now he sported skinny jeans and a Linkin Park T-shirt. He pulled his newly minted ID from a pocket and flushed the other fake ID down the toilet. He slipped his Glock G43X into the waist of his jeans and topped off his new look by donning a Washington Commanders cap with the brim in the back. He glanced at his transformation in the mirror.

*I should be okay unless I get stopped. Then it will depend on how well-trained the person who stops me will be.*

He knew he had to get out of the hospital as quickly as possible. He felt sure the arrival of the cadre of police meant Holmes' death had been discovered, but he also felt sure he had avoided security cameras.

He unlocked the door and glanced in both directions. There were still a few police moving around the lobby, but he decided boldness was his best move. He exited the men's room and moved to the main entrance, walking out without anyone stopping him. He felt a sudden vibration in the tight pocket of his jeans and struggled to pull out his 'last resort' cell phone.

*This can't be good*, he thought.

When he finally answered it, the woman on the other end of the call simply said, "They have a clear picture of you. Return to base as soon as possible."

No further instructions. He knew being captured was out of the question. It would mean that some way, somehow, he would meet the same end as Holmes.

*So I just have to get back to our base without being captured.* He walked out the front door of the hospital and laughed. *Looks like I'm clear.*

\* \* \*

Jordan and Detectives Solomon and Barnes examined the body camera recording of the officer guarding Holmes' room. Less than thirty minutes before, a young man dressed as a lab technician had entered Holmes' room, but they didn't have a clear view of his face. A few minutes later, they saw a full-face shot of the young man as he fist-bumped the police officer.

"We need to lock this place down. Get this picture to everyone you've got on-site, as well as hospital security. It's a big hospital. He can't have gotten far," Jordan said with a clear sense of urgency.

The detectives copied the image and circulated it among the other officers and to the head of hospital security, asking him to do the same.

Jordan copied it and sent it to Nadia and Martinez, then called Nadia. "Be on the lookout for this guy when you get here. He may be Holmes' killer."

* * *

"Is he armed?" Nadia asked, glancing at McKenna on the back floorboard.

"Unknown at this time. The hospital just went on lockdown, but he may still be in the vicinity."

"Understood," Nadia said right before Jordan ended the call.

Nadia memorized the face in the image, but she also knew clothing or other details may have been changed. Martinez pulled into the parking lot near the front of the hospital and parked in a spot marked "Reserved for Law Enforcement." They noticed they were joining several marked police cars at the scene, but they saw no uniformed officers near the front entrance.

"Jordan said the hospital is on lockdown. They're not out here because they're keeping everyone inside," Nadia said almost casually.

Then she noticed a young man come around the corner of the building. He was wearing skinny jeans, a T-shirt, and a backward ball cap, which gave her a clear view of his face.

"Oh, my God, it's him!" she said as she bumped Martinez's arm and pointed.

"Yep," he said, "I think you're right, Tosh."

They both slowly opened the doors to the SUV, hoping to appear like a couple who had come to visit someone in the hospital.

"Kenna," Nadia said before closing and locking her door, "stay down."

They were both assigned to McKenna's protection, but the best way they could protect her now was to keep her out of sight and take down this suspect. Their weapons were concealed within their jackets. As they approached the hospital, Martinez veered to the left so he could, hopefully, come up behind the suspect. Once he was in position, they both drew their weapons.

"NSA!" Nadia yelled at the man, who appeared startled. "Down on your knees and put your hands up!"

The man froze momentarily.

Martinez repeated Nadia's orders. "She said down on your knees and hands up! Now!"

The man turned to look at Martinez then looked back at Nadia. He was closer to Nadia. He slid his right hand under his T-shirt.

"Don't do it!" Nadia yelled again.

Without hesitation, he put the Glock in his mouth and pulled the trigger.

# Chapter 27

Mac had dozed off and woke up suddenly, wondering how long she had been asleep. She glanced at the clock on the opposite side of her room and was surprised to find that she had been asleep nearly two hours.

*Jordan must have forgotten about my coffee*, she thought with a sigh. The simple pleasure of a good cup of coffee would be so appreciated right now, and it didn't seem like a lot to ask for under the circumstances.

However, a few minutes later, Jordan came in with two cups of coffee—one he sipped on himself and her promised cup.

Mac smiled. "I thought you forgot."

"No chance," he said. "There have just been a few other developments, and I was just now able to get to the Best Brew kiosk downstairs to get it."

Mac frowned. "What other developments?"

Jordan handed her a cup of coffee and sat down in the chair beside the bed. He didn't answer right away, and Mac could tell he was weighing his words carefully.

"Okay," he finally said after another long sip. "I'll give you the short version, at least for now." He leaned forward in the chair. "Holmes, the man who tried to kill you on 295, was, we believe, murdered here in the hospital, probably by his own people."

Mac choked on her coffee. "Murdered?" she sputtered. "Oh, my God, Vernon!"

Jordan held up his right hand to signal a pause. "We got the murderer, Mac. He was taken down just outside the hospital. We've doubled the guard on both your room and Emma's, although I think Emma will be discharged soon."

"How...?" Mac started to ask, but Jordan stopped her.

"That's all I can tell you right now until the investigation is complete."

Mac frowned and took another sip of her coffee. She knew that caffeine was a stimulant, but at the moment, the taste and feel of her favorite drink felt somehow calming and comforting. She looked at Jordan with a weak smile. "Thanks for this," she said raising the cardboard cup. "It helps."

Jordan nodded. "You're welcome. Coffee wasn't the only request you made, though. You wanted to see your sister, too."

Mac's face brightened a little. "Is she here?"

"She is. Tosh and Martinez brought her to the hospital a couple of hours ago."

Mac was indignant. "A couple of hours ago? So where is she, Vernon?"

"Her visit to you was delayed because Tosh and Martinez were the ones who encountered Holmes' suspected killer when they arrived at the hospital."

"Where's Kenna, Vernon? Please tell me that she's okay!"

Jordan stood up and put his hand on Mac's shoulder. "Yes, she's okay, Mac," he assured her. "A bit shaken up by all the excitement, I think, and a little stiff from crouching on the floor of the SUV."

Mac looked puzzled. "Crouching on the floor? Was there gunfire?"

"No, well, not directed toward her or the SUV. Nadia's instincts are legendary, however, and she had McKenna put on a Kevlar vest and helmet and crouch on the floor as a precaution."

Mac released a sigh of relief. "When can I see her?"

"In a few minutes. She's out in the hall with Tosh and Martinez. I just wanted to bring you up to speed first, and I thought you needed to hear it from me. Are you ready?"

Mac nodded, and Jordan turned toward the door. "Vernon, before you go, what's my status?"

"We're working on that. I think we'll have an answer soon."

Mac nodded again, and Jordan opened the door. McKenna walked in still wearing the Kevlar vest and helmet with Nadia following close behind her.

"Well, look at you!" Mac said, hoping to coax a smile from her sister, and she did.

"Yeah, I look like some sort of commando, don't I?" McKenna said as she gestured to her gear.

Nadia moved closer to McKenna and smiled. "I don't think you need these here," she said. "I meant to put them back in the SUV before we came up, but there was a lot going on." She took the vest and helmet from McKenna, and their eyes seemed to lock on each other momentarily. She then touched McKenna on the shoulder. "I'll be right outside. I think you and your sister could use some privacy."

"Thanks, Nadia." McKenna smiled back.

Mac had felt something about the energy in the room shift during the exchange between the two of them. As Nadia left the room, McKenna leaned over and gave Mac a long but gentle hug before she sat down in the chair beside the bed.

McKenna looked over the visible parts of Mac's body and winced. "How are you, really?"

"I'm sore. I have a couple of broken ribs, a lot of bruising, and I got shot in the leg." Mac scrunched up her face in hopes of minimizing McKenna's concerns. "My leg is going to be okay, though, Kenna. The shot went straight through my calf without causing any severe damage."

"My God, Mac, you could have been killed."

"But I wasn't, Kenna. I'm still here." She reached for McKenna's hand.

McKenna accepted it and wiped a tear away with the other. "Is this ever going to be over?"

"Yeah, it will be, and soon I think—or at least Jordan seems to think so."

McKenna nodded and squeezed Mac's hand. "I hope so."

The two of them sat together quietly for several minutes in an effort to mutually digest all that had happened. Then Mac remembered the noticeable shift in energy as McKenna and Nadia had faced each other.

"So what's going on with you and Ziva David?" she finally asked with a smile.

\* \* \*

Russo, Marks, Richards, and Torro assisted the two men who had arrived with the truck. They knew the silent chopper wouldn't land until the truck departed, so they moved quickly. As they grabbed their last load, Richards stopped Torro on the way to the truck.

"Look, man," he whispered. "Something about this feels off to me."

"Yeah," Torro whispered back, "I've been feeling the same way." He turned to face his friend. "What do you want to do?"

"I don't know," Richards said, looking around to see if anyone had noticed them talking. "I'm not sure about Holmes dying in the line of duty, and I don't want to happen to us what happened to him, you know?"

"You mean you think the feds killed him?"

"Maybe," Richards whispered. "Maybe it wasn't the feds who killed him."

Torro looked horrified. "You think Agma killed him?"

Richards looked around again and gave Torro a light punch in the arm. "Keep your voice down, man!"

Torro raised his hand not holding equipment in a gesture of surrender.

"Don't you remember the Loyalty Oath we took when we joined up?"

Torro frowned. "Yeah, sort of. It seemed sort of a formality more than anything. Why?"

They heard Russo's voice coming through their coms. "He's reminding you of the Loyalty Oath because it includes an acknowledgment that no one ever leaves Agma."

Richards and Torro held their breath and stared at each other.

"I'll give you one pass on this. I will forget your conversation and the direction it seemed to be going because you're good men. I suggest, however, that you remember when your coms are live. I also suggest that you reconsider any thoughts of bailing out of this organization. Understood?"

Richards and Torro began to breathe again. "Understood, sir. Thank you, sir," they said in unison.

"Good," Russo replied. "Now get your asses in gear and finish loading the truck so we can get out of here."

* * *

Russo clicked off his coms and motioned for Marks to do the same. "Looks like we may have a couple of problems."

"Like you said, they're good men, Russo. I think they just got spooked about Holmes." He paused for a moment and looked for any listening ears nearby. "What are you going to do?"

Russo sighed. "Shit, I don't know." He ran his hand through his long dark hair. "I'm not sure it's my call. Maybe I should talk to the woman."

Mark's only response was his eyes suddenly opening much wider and his mouth gaping, but nothing came out. He and Russo had been part of the team with Richards and Torro for five years.

Russo sighed. "Look, man, if they try to cut and run, Agma will probably take us out, too. Do you want to take that risk? I don't." Russo pulled out his 'last resort' cell phone and walked away to get further instructions.

When the silent chopper arrived, all four men were on the chopper, but only Russo and Marks were still breathing. Richards and Torro had both been shot in the back of the head, their bodies wrapped in tarps, weighed down with large ammo boxes filled with rocks, and were dropped from the sky as the chopper made an arial U-turn in the middle of the Chesapeake Bay.

# Chapter 28

McKenna was trying to formulate an answer to Mac's question about what was going on with her and Nadia, but she wasn't quite sure how to articulate something she had never experienced before. She opened her mouth in a stumbling attempt to do so but was interrupted when Jordan walked back into the room.

"Hey," he said, "sorry to interrupt, but I thought you'd want to know. I just spoke with your doctor, and he says he's discharging you as soon as physical therapy gets a crutch up here for you."

Mac and McKenna both smiled.

"So, we can finally go home?" McKenna asked. "Mac, why don't you stay at my place until you're a little more mobile?"

Before Mac could respond, Jordan interrupted. "I'm sorry, but we're not prepared for either of you to go home yet. We need to take you back to the safe house for a little longer."

The sisters gave an exasperated sigh simultaneously.

"Why?" Mac asked, catching her breath. "Vick is dead. David is dead. The other guy who tried to kill me is dead, and the guy who killed him is dead. Is there someone else out there we need to be worried about?"

Jordan looked down, and his face tensed. "We're not sure about that right now, but that's not the only reason NSA wants you in the safe house." He paused for a moment. "They're still investigating you, Mac, and they won't allow you to leave the safe house until they're satisfied you're clear."

McKenna was too dumbstruck to say anything, but her expression said it all.

Mac rubbed her temples with her fingers. Then suddenly she raised her head to Jordan. "You're the head of Section 5, Jordan. Why aren't you there working on that? Working to help clear my name?" Her frustration shifted to anger. "I'm not a spy or a terrorist, Vernon. I'm a horn player! You know that!"

The door to Mac's hospital room still had a police officer posted both outside and inside. Jordan turned to the insider officer. "Ma'am, would you step outside the room, please?"

She frowned. "My orders are to remain just inside the door, sir."

Jordan was sympathetic but firm. "Yes, ma'am, that's true. I am, in fact, the one who requested that, but your detail has also been ordered to cooperate with NSA, which means with me, and I need to have a private conversation."

She was still frowning. "I understand, sir, but I still need to get the okay from our on-site commander."

Jordan nodded, and the officer called her supervisor and relayed Jordan's request. After receiving her supervisor's approval, she nodded to Jordan.

"I'll be just outside the door when you're ready for me to return, sir."

"Thank you," he said. "It won't take long." After she left the room, Jordan sat in a chair next to Mac's hospital bed, which allowed the three of them to see each other face-to-face.

No one spoke for a few minutes, then Mac threw her hands up and gave Jordan a look that said, *Well?*

He raised his hand and said, "Okay, okay," but it still took him a few moments to say anything further. "I've been taken out of the loop on the NSA's investigation of you."

Mac looked puzzled. "I don't understand. Why would they do that? You're the head of the section running this investigation." Her expression changed to one of surprise. "Do they think you're somehow involved?"

Jordan looked surprised by her question, but he also seemed to relax a little. "No, they don't have any concerns about me. My whole life has been an open book to them for years."

"So then why, Vernon?" Mac frowned.

"My life has been an open book to NSA for years, but it hasn't been an open book to the two of you."

Mac and McKenna glanced at each other then back to Jordan.

"Us?" Mac asked. "Why should it be?"

Jordan took a deep breath. "They don't allow family to investigate family—and I'm part of your family." He paused for a moment and looked at each of them. "I'm your uncle."

Both women were so shocked at his statement that they had no response.

"When I started my career in intelligence, I worked undercover. The backstory they created for me was that my parents were dead, and I had no other living family members. It was just safer that way—safer for your parents and safer for the two of you. Your parents weren't happy about it, but they were analysts for the agency. They understood—and they wanted to keep you safe," He leaned forward in his chair, becoming more comfortable for his long-awaited disclosure. "When I left undercover work and advanced in the agency, my work became less of a threat to my family, and we saw each other occasionally."

"Yeah, I remember you kind of being around for backyard cookouts and things like that when we were teenagers," Mac said.

McKenna slowly nodded before the sudden realization hit her. "They always called you Mr. Jordan. You mean you're actually *Uncle* Vernon?"

Jordan smiled. "That I am. I am your mother's older brother."

It was McKenna's turn to look puzzled. "But Mom's family name wasn't Jordan."

He nodded. "You're right. It wasn't. When I left undercover work, I dropped my alias, but it still didn't feel safe for me to go back to the family name, so I chose a new name. My first and last names are a combination of names pulled from farther back in our family tree, but I've been Vernon Jordan for so long now, I could never be comfortable with anything else."

"So why tell us now—after all of this time?" Mac asked.

"First of all, I finally have permission to share the information. Second, I thought it might help you, Mac, understand some of the reasons I pulled you into my section when all of this started to unfold. I wanted to make sure you were safe. And three," he paused for a moment, "I think at this point in my life—and maybe in yours, too—it would be nice to know that we have family."

Mac and McKenna were quiet.

"Look," he finally said, "I know this is a lot to take in, so I'm going to leave the two of you to think about it, talk about it, and then maybe we can talk about it together again." He got up to leave.

As he reached the door, Mac said, "Thank you for telling us, Vernon. It wasn't easy to hear, but I also realize it probably wasn't easy to say."

Jordan smiled. "Actually," he said, his hand on the open door, "it gives me a tremendous sense of relief. I just hope the two of you can forgive the secrecy—from me and from your parents. I'll see you at the safe house." He then exited the room, and they heard him tell the inside officer that she could resume her post.

Mac and McKenna looked into each other's eyes for several minutes, communicating not specific thoughts in some mystical, telepathic way, but communicating a range of feelings with each other that neither of them could quite articulate.

# Chapter 29

As Jordan walked out of Mac's hospital room, his cell phone rang. He recognized the number of NSA Deputy Director Clement. "Jordan," he answered.

"We've all been busy here for the past several days, Vernon. I know you've been concerned about Hollingsworth's status, but I think we may be able to clear her," Clement said without identifying himself.

Jordan stopped walking. "May be able to, sir?"

"Yes," Clement continued. "What is her status at the hospital?"

"I spoke with her doctor a few minutes ago. He plans to discharge her today. I just told her and informed her and her sister that they would need to go back to the safe house until we were certain she wasn't involved in this threat."

"Okay, but rather than taking them to the safe house, I'd like for you to bring them here. I know she's injured, but it shouldn't take long."

"What you have in mind, sir?"

"Because of your relationship with her, I think it's best that you find out when she does. I know that's not the answer you wanted, but I think you will understand when all of this is said and done."

Jordan had been with the agency long enough to know not to press anymore for an answer. "Okay. When do you want us to be there?"

"At two o'clock this afternoon, if her doctor can discharge her by then."

"I'll see to it, sir."

Clement ended the call. Jordan was good at reading people, but he couldn't get a good read on Clement from their phone conversation. However, he had said that whatever this meeting was about, it may involve clearing Mac of any part in the threat created by David and Agma.

He turned around and headed back to the nurses' station and found Mac's doctor still typing notes into one of the computers.

"Dr. Cook," he began, "I'm sorry to interrupt you, but I just spoke with my boss. He would like me to take Ms. Hollingsworth to a meeting at our office at two o'clock. Is that doable?"

Dr. Cook looked at his watch and raised his eyebrows. "It's almost noon. It will require pulling some strings to get physical therapy up here with her crutch, but I think we can make that work."

Jordan nodded. "Thank you, Doc."

"I noticed that her sister came in to see her. I doubt that either one of them is likely to be happy with the default lunch tray that will arrive soon. Why don't you inform them of the change in plans and pick up something more satisfying for them? I'll speak with the head of PT and ask them to come up no later than one. Will that give you enough time to get where you need to go?"

"It will be tight, but I will make it happen."

"Very good." Dr. Cook took out his cell phone and called his friend Al, who headed up the PT department.

Jordan turned and headed back to Mac's room. Both she and McKenna were surprised to see him again.

"There's been a change in plans," he told them. "I've been asked to take you to NSA for a meeting at two o'clock. Dr. Cook is making arrangements for PT to come up sooner so they can get you out of here. Meanwhile, I'm going to go downstairs and grab lunch for both of you. I think I saw a Subway sandwich place down there. Is that okay?"

"Whoa," Mac said, shaking her head. "Let's back up for a minute. Why do they need me at NSA? What kind of meeting?"

"Unfortunately, I wasn't given any details, Mac. However, Clement did say that this meeting could help clear you of any involvement in this threat."

Mac frowned and looked at McKenna, who was also frowning. "What about Kenna?" she asked, facing Jordan again.

"Clement didn't specifically say so, but I'm planning to take her with us. If they don't want her in the meeting, she can wait outside the conference room."

The sisters looked at each other again, and for the second time in fifteen minutes, Jordan had trouble reading someone—both of them, in fact.

"I am a little hungry, and it sounds like you don't know how long we'll be there, so, yeah, Subway is okay. I'll take a cheesesteak and a Diet Coke," Mac concluded.

McKenna said, "Yeah, I'll have the same."

Jordan turned to Officer Woodward, who was back at her post just inside the door. "Anything for you, Officer?"

"No, thanks. It's kind of you to ask, but I can't eat while standing my post."

"Of course. I should have known that. It's been quite a day, and I just didn't consider it."

Dr. Cook was true to his word, and no sooner than the sisters had finished their lunch, a physical therapist arrived with crutches for Mac, made some adjustments, and instructed her on how to use them.

While PT was working with Mac, Jordan called Tosh and Martinez to tell them of the change in plans. He told them they would take the sisters in their SUV and follow him back to NSA. When they arrived, Jordan had someone waiting with a wheelchair for Mac, and, in spite of her embarrassment about using it, she didn't protest.

Jordan, Mac, McKenna, Tosh, and Martinez all cleared security and took the elevator down to Sublevel 3. Jordan walked ahead of the group to seek out Deputy Director Clement and found him in the conference room. Clement and Sullivan were both seated at the conference table with a man Jordan had never seen before. They all looked up as Jordan entered. Then Clement and Sullivan both rose, and Sullivan addressed the stranger at the table.

"Excuse us for a few minutes, Mr. Drummer," he said. "We need to brief our agent, and we'll be back with you shortly. Can we get you anything? Coffee? Soda?"

"Just a cup of water, please," the man replied without looking at Clement or Sullivan.

Sullivan, Clement, and Jordan stepped out into the hall, and Clement instructed Martinez to get the man a glass of water. Then he motioned with his head to a room next door to the conference room. As Jordan entered the room with his two bosses, he found two men and two women seated at a long table that faced a one-way window that provided a view of the conference room.

"I think you already know these folks, don't you, Vernon?" Clement asked.

Jordan recognized James Powell from Forensic Accounting; Dr. Elizabeth Berry, NSA's best profiler; Alister Armstrong from Cyber Security; and Dr. Alice Robbins, NSA's head Psychologist.

"Of course." Jordan nodded to the four. "I've worked with all of them at one time or another." His four colleagues nodded back in a return greeting.

"Have a seat, Jordan," Sullivan said as he and Clement both pulled out chairs to seat themselves.

Jordan also sat down. "I know everyone here except the man in the conference room, and I have to say I'm curious about the combination of expertise in this room." He pointed to the man at the conference table. "He's somehow involved in all of this?"

Everyone looked to Sullivan for how to proceed.

To Jordan's surprise, Sullivan smiled—a rare occurrence. "Yes, I guess you could say he's involved, but not in the way any of us could have imagined."

Jordan noticed that the others were also smiling, which left him even more perplexed.

Sullivan turned to Clement. "Paul," he said, "why don't you take it from here?"

Clement turned to Jordan. "Vernon," he said, "we're all so used to dealing with people of questionable character, criminals, killers, terrorists." He waved his hand to indicate that the list could be longer. "But what you see before you at the conference table is an honest man with a spotless history. He's never even had a parking ticket."

Clement paused for a moment. "Our best experts have turned this man's life inside out and found nothing that would raise any concerns, especially no concerns about terrorism or national security."

Sullivan picked up the briefing again. "This gentleman is Mez Drummer. He's an attorney in Annapolis specializing in trusts, wills, and estates. His colleagues have nothing but praise for him. He's well respected not only for his legal work but also for his charity work. Mr. Drummer is actually a drummer—in a cover band that plays charity gigs all over the state." Sullivan stopped to take a sip of the coffee that had been waiting for him on the table. "Our interest in Mr. Drummer was that he was David Lindsey's attorney."

# Chapter 30

The pilot of the silent chopper radioed the woman he only knew as JoAnn at Agma headquarters to request she open the roof access so he could land. As they approached, he, Russo, and Marks watched as the giant sliding door opened. Its camouflage was perfect—almost as invisible on the ground as it was from the air. The pilot landed the chopper, and the great door closed again.

As they exited the helicopter, Russo and Marks were greeted by an armed guard who didn't introduce himself.

All he said was, "She wants to see you." Then he motioned for them to follow him.

Russo had spoken to the woman many times but had never met her. He once thought she was merely a radio operator who managed communications to operatives in the field, but he had heard rumors that her role was more important. They never included any specifics.

The massive complex they were in was housed in a remote mountain area in West Virginia. He had often wondered how they kept the location a secret for so long, then Holmes had told him that Agma had purchased hundreds of acres in the surrounding area so their organization would be able to do their work without being bothered by hikers, curiosity seekers, or government officials.

The guard directed them through a suite of offices to a large office on the opposite side of the room. He knocked and heard "Enter," then opened the door for Russo and Marks to enter the room. He then shut the door again and remained outside, awaiting further instructions.

Russo and Marks looked around the elegantly appointed office that included a long conference table, a wall full of monitors, and a large oak desk that appeared to be hand-carved. Behind the desk stood a woman he judged to be in her fifties, with short brown hair. She wore fatigues that weren't exactly tight but fit her frame in a way that made it clear she spent a lot of time working out. When she finally spoke, he recognized her voice and knew she was the one he had spoken to on his 'last resort' phone. He also knew this was not the office of a radio operator.

"Sit down," she said, gesturing to the two plush armchairs in front of her desk.

Both men complied, and the woman sat down behind the desk.

"The two of you have done well. Even though things didn't go as planned, we are very pleased with your performance.

"Thank you, ma'am," they said in unison.

"We would like the two of you to become part of a new task force whose job will be to design a new mission to achieve Agma's goals. Your participation in this task force will, of course, include an increase in your compensation and an opportunity to move into positions of greater command within the organization."

Russo and Marks were both stunned, but managed to get out another, "Thank you, ma'am."

"I can assume then that you are both willing to accept this assignment?"

"Yes, ma'am," they said again in unison.

"I'm glad to have you on board, gentlemen." She paused for a moment and had a faraway look in her eyes. "The death of James Vick was a huge loss. Unfortunately, he took some risks I wish—that we wish—he hadn't taken." She paused again, and Russo could have sworn she was struggling to contain her emotions. "But what is past is past," she finally said. "We must move on. We must continue the project we devised many years ago and eliminate the threats to our country in ways that our government will not."

She stood up and paced around the office, looking at what seemed to be personal objects or pictures on the bookshelves next to the wall of monitors. Russo and Marks glanced at each other with an unspoken question about whether they should speak, but they chose not to. The woman eventually turned around and walked back toward her desk. Instead of taking a seat behind it, though, she stood in front of it, facing the two men. She held out her hand in an invitation for a handshake. Both men instantly rose from their seats and took turns shaking her hand.

"Welcome to the inner circle of Agma, gentlemen. My name is JoAnn Vick. James Vick was my husband." She gestured toward the door. "Please hold any questions for another time. The guard outside the door will show you to your new quarters."

Russo and Marks tried unsuccessfully to hide their shock at this revelation, but they both recovered enough to nod and say, "Yes, ma'am," before they exited the office.

\* \* \*

Alone once again, JoAnn sat down at her desk and rubbed her eyes and the bridge of her nose. It wasn't supposed to be like this. She and James had planned all of this together. They had worked to raise the funds they needed to start the organization, build a secure headquarters, and implement plans to put an end to threats to the country in ways they knew the government would never do. Now she found herself at the head of the organization—an organization that had sustained significant losses during this failed mission. And the man she had loved, respected, and worked closely with for twenty years was gone.

She tapped a few keys to wake up her computer, entered her password, and opened an image on her desktop. A woman in a Navy uniform with flaming red hair stared back at her, holding a French Horn in front of her.

*How much of a role did she play in the failure of this mission? Would James be alive now if she had not been involved?*

They had tried to kill her several times, considering her a loose end. Was she? Was it worth trying again? JoAnn knew Hollingsworth had stumbled into their mission because of bad choices made by David. JoAnn closed the image.

*I'm not sure what to do about you, MacKenzie Hollingsworth, but I can't think about that right now. There are too many other things that need doing to get us back on track. Perhaps I will think more about this later.*

# Chapter 31

Jordan was shocked at Sullivan's revelation, but he was also confused about why everyone seemed to be smiling. "You've already questioned him?"

"Not exactly," Sullivan said. "We didn't bring Mr. Drummer in. He contacted us and said he had important information to share about David Lindsey." Sullivan motioned to the others in the room. "We've all heard his story already, and everything he said has checked out. We have all concluded that he is telling the truth. However, we would like to see Hollingsworth's reaction to his story."

Clement added, "That's why I didn't want to disclose anything to you on the phone, Vernon. We didn't want to run the risk that you would inadvertently say anything that might prepare her."

Jordan frowned. He didn't like the implication of Clement's comments, but he also knew Clement was doing his job. He shrugged. "Okay," he said, "so now what happens?"

"What happens now," Sullivan said, "is that you and Clement will go back in there with Mr. Drummer, Hollingsworth, and her sister. I will remain here with our panel of experts to observe."

"One thing worth noting," added Dr. Robbins, "Mr. Drummer is on the autism spectrum, so you may find his way of being a little different."

Jordan wasn't sure what she meant by that, but he nodded anyway.

Clement rose, and Jordan followed him out of the observation room and into the hall where Mac, McKenna, Martinez, and Tosh were waiting. Clement asked Martinez and Tosh to wait and motioned for the two sisters to follow him and Jordan into the conference room.

Drummer didn't move or look up when they came back in. He seemed to be busy arranging several documents on the table in front of him. He did look up when Clement spoke to him.

"Mr. Drummer, we're sorry to keep you waiting." He then introduced Jordan, Mac, and MacKenna. "They've all come to hear what you've already told us about David Lindsey."

Drummer nodded.

Then Jordan said, "I'm sorry that your client is dead, Mr. Drummer. Did you know Mr. Lindsey well?"

Drummer cocked his head. "Yes, I knew him for several years. Would you like for me to begin?" Drummer looked at Mac. "And you are MacKenzie Hollingsworth?"

"Yes, sir, that's correct," Mac said.

Drummer paused again, looking at no one in particular. "I'm sorry. I'm feeling a bit anxious. I'm not usually in a meeting with this many people."

"Yes," Jordan said, "I understand that you have some sort of disability?"

"I do?" Drummer said with a curious expression.

Jordan tried to clarify. "Yes, they told me that you are on the autism spectrum."

"Oh, that." Drummer gestured with his hand as if he were shooing away a fly. "Yes, I am, but I don't consider that a disability, Mr. Jordan. I just do things a little differently than many people do."

Jordan rarely felt embarrassed, but he could feel his face turning a deep red. "I'm sorry, sir," he said. "I meant no disrespect."

"Thank you," Drummer said. "Shall I begin?"

Clement responded, "Yes, of course, whenever you're ready."

Drummer took a deep breath. "Let me start by saying that I have David's written permission to reveal the things I am telling you. David did some things he shouldn't have done, and he regretted doing them. He never told me what he had done because he didn't want to implicate me. Recently, however, he contacted me and instructed me to do several things on his behalf because he was involved in something dangerous and did not expect to survive. He gave me his account number for a bank in the Cayman Islands. He told me this account held several million dollars he had earned illegally. He told me that, if he died, I was to turn the information over to the government. I have already done so."

Drummer paused for a few moments then took a few deep breaths before continuing. "David told me that when he started to earn this illegal money, he lived off some of it in cash and put the rest in the bank. When he started living off the illegal money, he let his paychecks from the Navy accumulate in his account at the Bank of Laurel. All the money he has in that account is money he earned legally as a French Horn player in the Navy Band. David received some wise investment advice from a woman he knew at the bank, and, over the years, the account grew to over three million dollars." Drummer took another break and another few deep breaths.

"When he contacted me recently, he made a few changes in his will. The change that is most relevant to this meeting today is that he put the three million dollars in his will as a trust." He turned to Mac. "He named you, Ms. Hollingsworth, as temporary trustee. The trust stipulates that the money is to be used for the two children a woman named Ann Headley left behind. I understand she died recently."

Mac, McKenna, and Jordan's jaws all dropped at once, but Mac was the only one who finally spoke. "What?" she said. "He named me as the temporary trustee? David and I hardly knew each other!"

Drummer nodded, but his expression didn't change. "Yes, David told me you didn't know each other very well, but David didn't have any friends or family. He said he had been a loner all his life. He made you temporary trustee because he thought you were a good and trustworthy person. If you don't want the responsibility, the trust allows you to name another person or persons as permanent trustees."

Mac seemed stunned. "I wouldn't have any idea who to name! I didn't know Ann at all!" She looked at MacKenna, who was eager to jump in.

"I knew Ann. I know her children. I know her ex-husband. He's a wonderful father, Mac."

Mac gestured toward David's lawyer. "Mr. Drummer, can you take care of that? Can you make Ann Headley's ex-husband the trustee?"

"Yes, of course," Drummer said. "I just need his name and contact information—and then his acceptance of that responsibility."

McKenna said, "I can provide you with the information. I've known him for years. I can't imagine he would not accept it."

"That sounds like a perfect solution," Jordan added. "Is everyone on board with it?"

McKenna nodded, and Mac said, "Absolutely!"

Drummer cocked his head and said almost to himself, "The use of *onboard* is an idiomatic metaphor for verifying consensus." He paused in thought for a moment before adding, "Yes, I believe we have a consensus. I will contact this man and inform you, Ms. Hollingsworth, when you are no longer involved in the trust."

Mac sighed. "Thank you, Mr. Drummer."

McKenna smiled. She knew that Brian, the father of Annie's children, would have made sure their needs were met in the best way he could on his own, but the trust would provide even more financial security for them in the future.

The room was suddenly quiet as everyone struggled with all the information Drummer had shared. In the observation room, Sullivan and his panel of experts agreed they were satisfied with their investigation of Mac, as well as her reaction to the information Drummer shared, and concluded that she had, indeed, stumbled into all of this because she had discovered the vial David had hidden in her horn—just as she had always maintained.

# Chapter 32

Sullivan and his panel of experts exited the observation room as Jordan opened the door to the conference room. McKenna was giving Mr. Drummer Brian Headley's contact information, and Mac thanked him for taking care of the change.

"David was a good client. I'm sorry he is dead," he responded, though his facial expression showed no obvious emotion. He finished gathering up his documents and Brian's contact information, put them neatly into his briefcase, and then walked toward the door. "Good day," he said before Jordan instructed Martinez to escort him out of the building.

Jordan was about to join McKenna and Mac as they walked toward the door, but Sullivan walked up beside him. He was on his cell phone and held up his free hand to pause Jordan's movement.

"Yes, ma'am," he said to the person on the other end of the call. "I can have them there within the hour." Jordan guessed the pause that followed was because the call had not yet ended. Then he heard Sullivan say, "Thank you, ma'am. We appreciate your support."

Sullivan ended the call and turned to Jordan as Clement walked up to join them. "The issue of Ms. Hollingsworth's involvement is now officially closed. We're not getting any chatter about Agma, so we don't know what, if anything, may still develop with them, but she is clear."

Jordan gave a sigh of relief, and he and Clement shook hands.

"Good work on this case, Vernon," Clement said.

"Thank you, Tom," Jordan responded. Neither of them moved, however, because Sullivan remained with them. "Was there something else, sir?" Jordan asked.

"Yes, as a matter of fact, there is. I just got off the phone with the president. She has, of course, been fully briefed on this crisis and would like to meet with Ms. Hollingsworth before she has to leave for the Climate Change Summit in Paris, which means that we need to get her over there within the hour. I need both of you to make that happen."

Clement and Jordan both raised their eyebrows in surprise, then Jordan interrupted Mac and McKenna's discussion about the trust and how much it would mean for Annie's children.

"We've got to go—now!" he said, taking control of Mac's wheelchair as they moved to the elevator with a stunned McKenna on one side and Clement on the other.

They all moved into the elevator, and Jordan pressed the button for the ground floor while Clement was on his cell phone, arranging what sounded like emergency transportation.

Mac threw up her hands and was instantly reminded of her broken ribs. "What's going on?"

Jordan turned to face her and said, "There's another meeting we have to take you to, and we have to be there within the hour." He paused as he looked at the scrubs the hospital had given her when she was discharged. "You're not going to be happy about what you're wearing, but you're about to meet the president of the United States."

McKenna was speechless, but Mac managed a shocked response, "What? Why?" She looked at Jordan, "Am I in trouble again? I thought this was over!"

Jordan patted her gently on the shoulder before the elevator stopped, and they exited toward the front entrance of the building where two more black SUVs were waiting.

"No," Jordan said. "You're not in trouble. All I know is that the president was fully briefed on this whole episode and wanted to meet with you before she has to leave for the summit in Paris."

"Dressed like this?" she exclaimed.

"Those were our orders, Mac. Sorry." He smiled. "It'll be okay. I've met her once or twice. She's a surprisingly down-to-earth person."

Mac threw up her hands. "Well, that's great to know, Vernon," she said, her frustration growing, "but I can't go to the White House and meet the president in scrubs!"

Jordan's expression grew more serious, and he leaned over. "Mac, your Commander in Chief has requested your presence within the hour. She is aware of your current status—and your attire."

Mac frowned and looked away but finally turned back to Jordan and nodded as Martinez opened the door of the SUV to help her get in. Tosh was in the front passenger seat. McKenna entered through the other side and sat next to Mac. Jordan and Clement took the second SUV.

"I wished she'd given us a little more time, "Clement said. "This is going to be tight."

Jordan was driving, and both he and his boss were aware they were exceeding the speed limit for 295, just as they had instructed Martinez to do. It was midday in the middle of the week, and they made good time until they entered DC city limits. Clement radioed the other SUV.

"Use your lights and siren. We're running out of time."

Martinez and Jordan both engaged their blue lights and sirens. They all knew this was a violation of procedure, but Clement had issued the order, and he would be the one to explain the decision to Sullivan if necessary. Under the circumstances, he didn't think it would be.

They arrived at the White House gate with twenty minutes to spare and were quickly cleared to enter and park just outside the entrance to the West Wing. A Secret Service officer met them there to escort them to the Oval Office. Jordan pushed Mac's wheelchair as Clement walked alongside them through the wide hallways. Martinez, Tosh, and McKenna followed. No one spoke.

Mac, McKenna, Martinez, and Tosh all seemed to sense the history and significance of their surroundings and the gravity of a personal invitation. Clement and Jordan had been there several times over the years, but they, too, remained respectfully quiet.

The entourage stopped when the Secret Service agent held up his hand and said, "Please wait here." He then spoke to his colleague inside the Oval Office. "Ms. Hollingsworth is here." He must have received a response because he opened the door and instructed them all to enter.

❦ ❦ ❦

President Barbara Holton rose from behind the Resolute Desk and greeted them with a smile. She was not an especially tall woman, but she carried herself in a polished, regal way that made her appear taller than she was. The waves of her dark, salt-and-pepper hair made what was probably a carefully crafted style appear almost casual and effortless—and suited her well. She wore a white silk blouse under a cobalt blue suit that brought out the blue in her eyes. She motioned toward the sofas and chairs in the middle of the room and asked them to sit down. Jordan parked Mac's wheelchair in the space provided when the Secret Service agent removed one of the armchairs. President Holton took the armchair on the opposite side.

"I appreciate your willingness to come so quickly. I must leave shortly for Paris, but I wanted the opportunity to meet with you to bring some official closure to this episode—an episode in which you all performed very well, indeed." She looked around the circle at each of her seated guests. "You have my sincere thanks." She paused for a moment. "Unfortunately, because of the classified nature of these events, you will never receive the thanks or acknowledgment you deserve in a broader context."

She turned to Mac and McKenna. "If you have not already done so, I'm sure Mr. Clement and Mr. Jordan will go over the importance of you understanding and signing the Classified Information Non-Disclosure Agreement."

Clement responded, "Yes, ma'am. We will take care of that."

"Very well." She looked at her watch and then stood. Everyone else did as well, except for Mac. "If the rest of you will wait outside, I would like to speak to the Hollingsworths privately."

Mac and McKenna looked anxiously at each other as everyone else in their party left the room. The Secret Service agent posted inside the Oval Office remained after closing the door.

The President gestured to the agent and turned toward Mac and McKenna. "This is Special Agent Jan Mason. She rarely leaves my side," she said with a laugh, "and she will remain with us, of course."

Holton sat back down, and so did McKenna. "I understand that the two of you became involved in all of this through no fault of your own, and I'm sorry that happened." She turned to face Mac directly. "Nevertheless, you played a pivotal role in resolving this situation, and that role required significant sacrifices for you, which, I understand, you made willingly." She smiled. "You are an honor to the uniform and to your oath, Ms. Hollingsworth."

Mac met Holton's gaze and said, "Thank you, ma'am."

Holton nodded. "Thank *you*." She glanced at Mac's scrubs and smiled. "I understand you resisted the idea of coming here in scrubs."

Mac sighed. "Yes, ma'am. I felt like I should have been in uniform."

Holton waved her hand. "Let that go, Ms. Hollingsworth. What I want to know is: is there anything I can do for you?"

Mac seemed surprised by the question. "I would never ask for special treatment or a favor from you, ma'am. That wouldn't feel right to me."

"I expected you would say that," Holton said. She handed Mac a card with a cell phone number on it. "This number is answered twenty-four hours a day. If you should ever need it, please don't hesitate to use it."

"Thank you, ma'am."

Holton glanced at her watch again and then addressed both of the sisters. "What's next for the two of you?"

Mac and McKenna looked at each other for a moment, then Mac spoke for both of them. "We just want our lives and our jobs back, ma'am, so I guess we'll both start working toward that."

Holton cocked her head. "I'm sorry, perhaps no one has had a chance to inform you yet, but both of you will be returning to your jobs as soon as you're ready."

"I'm officially back in the Navy?" Mac said in disbelief. "And in the Navy Band?"

"Yes, of course." Holton said, "And you, McKenna—may I call you McKenna?" McKenna nodded. "You will return to your work as well." Holton allowed that information to sink in for a moment, then added, "Your coworkers must never know where you've been or what you've been doing. Mr. Clement will go over all of that with you. NSA will craft a plausible back story for you, McKenna, and will coach you on it until you're comfortable with it. Mac—may I call you Mac?" Mac nodded. "Your back story will be that you were on a special, classified assignment. Your colleagues have been instructed not to question you about it."

Mac smiled and tried not to chuckle. "I'm sorry, ma'am, but they're all going to wonder what kind of special, classified assignment would require a French Horn player."

"I'm sure they will," Holton responded with a smile. "Let them wonder." She glanced at her watch again. "McKenna and MacKenzie," she said thoughtfully. "Some Scottish ancestry, perhaps?"

"Yes, ma'am, especially on our mother's side. Genealogy was an interest of hers. She got our names from somewhere along the family tree," Mac said.

Holton smiled. "Then that's something else we have in common. A large percentage of my DNA comes from Scotland, too."

"Yes," Mac said. "I remember reading you were in the Navy, too—that you went to the Academy, I think?"

Holton sat back in her chair. "Yes, that's correct. I went to the Academy when female cadets were still a 'new and scary thing.'" She emphasized that with air quotes. "But that isn't the only other thing we have in common, either." She took a deep breath. "I knew your parents." She paused a moment until the shocked expressions on Mac and McKenna's faces normalized.

"My last five years in the Navy, I was assigned to NSA. I met my husband there. I also met your parents there. Our three-letter agencies are like small communities in many ways. I knew your mother better than I did your father. She and I became good friends."

"They never told us they knew you," McKenna said.

"I wouldn't have expected them to. That wasn't how things were handled at the agency then. Sometimes, they still aren't." She looked down. "Then I left the Navy and began my political career, and we sort of lost touch with each other, as old friends often do, unfortunately." She looked at each of the sisters. "When I learned how and why your parents died, though, I wished we had kept in touch. After my briefing on your involvement in this dreadful episode, I knew I had to meet you. Your parents would have been very proud of the fine women you've both become."

Agent Mason spoke for the first time since they had arrived. "Ma'am," she said and tapped her watch. "Marine One is here for you."

Holton stood up, followed by McKenna. "I have to go now," Holton said, "but I hope we have other opportunities to talk in the future." She gave them each a gentle hug and walked out the door.

# Chapter 33

Mac struggled to exit the room in her wheelchair on her own until Jordan saw her and stepped in to help.

"I can do this," Mac said stubbornly.

"Yeah," McKenna added, "She wouldn't let me help her."

"We know you can do it, but you don't have to. I've got this," Jordan said.

"Where are you taking us now, Vernon?" Mac asked with an edgy chuckle. "To the Pentagon?"

Jordan smiled. "No, you're done with meetings for today. I'm going to take you both to the safe house to retrieve any personal belongings you left there, and then I'm taking you both home."

"No more safe house?" McKenna asked tentatively.

"No more safe house," Jordan said. "Sullivan says there's no chatter we can find anywhere about Agma right now. We're guessing they're regrouping somewhere to plan their next moves."

"So you think we'll be safe at home now?" McKenna asked.

"Yes, we think so," Jordan said as they moved toward the West Wing exit. "If we learn anything that suggests otherwise, we'll take the necessary steps to ensure your safety."

McKenna hadn't noticed that Martinez and Tosh were missing until they stepped outside of the White House. "Where are Martinez and Nadia?" she asked. She had assumed they would be waiting with the SUV, but they weren't.

"We sent them home to get a little rest," Jordan said. "They'll be assigned a new case tomorrow."

"They're gone?" McKenna exclaimed. "But we didn't even get to thank them or tell them goodbye!"

At first, Jordan seemed surprised at the strength of McKenna's emotions about two people she had only known for a few days. "I'm sorry, McKenna," he said. "I guess we weren't thinking about that. I will try to make arrangements for you to do that another time if it's important to you."

McKenna frowned. "No, it's okay. I guess it's not that important."

Mac gave her sister a quizzical look. McKenna responded by just shaking her head. McKenna was quiet as Jordan drove them back to the safe house, but Mac and Jordan found plenty to talk about.

"Vernon, did you know that President Holton knew our parents? And that she and our mother were actually good friends while they were all at NSA?"

"Wow," he said, surprise evident on his face. "No, I didn't. She told you that, huh?"

"Yes, she did," Mac said. "She said they lost touch after she left NSA."

"Well," Jordan said, "I was working undercover at the time. I wasn't at headquarters much, and when I was, I never saw any of them. We were in completely different sections. Later on, I guess they didn't mention it because it was one of those things we all had learned to keep to ourselves."

"Yeah, she said something kind of like that." Then Mac changed the subject. "You know, I'm not sure we have anything we need to get at the safe house, Vernon. We didn't take anything with us."

McKenna jumped in. "I have a shirt there I'd like to get. I spilled coffee on it and washed it while I was there. It's just an old flannel shirt, but it's one of my favorites."

"I wondered why you were wearing a T-shirt," Mac said. "You've had that flannel shirt for years. So where did you get the T-shirt?"

McKenna looked out the window, not wanting Mac to see her face. "Nadia loaned it to me. How am I going to give it back to her?"

"Not a problem, McKenna," Jordan said casually. "I'll be glad to return it for you."

"Oh, okay," she said, looking out the window again. "I'll need to wash it first."

"Well, it's not like we won't see each other again," he said, "At least I hope not. I was hoping, now that you both know we are related, we could spend a little time together."

McKenna finally turned toward Mac with a 'well, what do you think?' look on her face.

Mac smiled. "You know, we've thought for so long that we had no other family. It's going to take a while to get used to the fact that we do." She paused and met McKenna's eyes. "But I think that would be a good thing, Vernon—maybe for all three of us."

"I think so, too," McKenna added.

"Thanks," Jordan said. "I think you're right."

They arrived at the safe house, and Jordan offered to go in and get McKenna's shirt. She told him she'd rather do it herself because she wanted to change back into it. So Jordan gave her the key code and told her how to both turn off and reset the alarm system.

"Maybe you better come with me," she said. "I don't want to push the wrong code in and have a bunch of black SUVs converging on us."

"You okay, Mac?" Jordan asked.

"Sure," she said. "We're only talking about a few minutes."

Jordan entered the key code to unlock the door and turned off the alarm. "Okay," he assured McKenna with a smile, "no converging black SUVs. Everything appears to be in order. I'll just wait here."

"Thanks. I'll just be a minute."

McKenna made her way through the living room, but when she reached the kitchen, she paused a moment, remembering her interaction with Nadia and how she felt being around her.

*Maybe she didn't feel the same way*, she thought. *She didn't even say goodbye.*

She sighed and continued through the kitchen to the laundry room. She expected to find her shirt in the dryer where she'd left it, but she found it lightly pressed on the only hanger dangling from the shelf above the washer and dryer.

*I guess they have a housekeeper who comes in and does things like that. That's really nice.*

She slipped Nadia's T-shirt off, took her flannel shirt off the hanger, and put it on. It felt comfortable and familiar, and she felt like even a small thing like having her favorite shirt back provided a welcome feeling of normalcy—something she and Mac had not had for several days.

As she finished buttoning up the shirt, she noticed a small piece of paper in one of the pockets. She pulled it out and read

*Coffee date? Call me when you're ready. Nadia 240-555-6921*

McKenna surprised herself by laughing out loud while also feeling a rush of warmth run through her body.

"You okay back there?" Jordan called to her.

"Yep!" she said as she emerged from the back of the house with a wide smile on her face and Nadia's T-shirt in her hand.

"Wow," Jordan said. "You really do love that shirt, don't you?" He reset the alarm, and they joined Mac back in the SUV. "Where to?" he asked. "Or have you decided yet?"

Mac looked at McKenna. "I appreciate you offering to let me stay at your place for a while, Kenna. I am pretty tired and need some Tylenol, but I'd like to go home tomorrow. I haven't touched my horn in days, and I really need that."

McKenna smiled. "Sure, Mac" she said. "I'd like for us to have some time to talk." Then she remembered something she hadn't thought about for days. "Neither of us have a car, though. Yours is gone." The smile disappeared. "Gone—with Annie." She took a deep breath. "And I don't know where mine is. I haven't seen it since we drove to the Maryland State Police office."

Jordan gestured with his hand. "I'll take care of that. I'll make sure someone drops your car off at your place tomorrow, McKenna."

"Okay, then," Mac said. "I guess we'll go to Kenna's place."

# Chapter 34

When they arrived at McKenna's house, Jordan went to the back of the SUV to get the wheelchair out for Mac.

"Oh, no," she said. "I'm not using that thing. The crutches will do just fine, thank you."

Jordan shrugged and closed the hatchback then attempted to help Mac get out of the vehicle.

"I've got this, Vernon," she assured him. "Please let me do this on my own. I've been pushed around enough."

Jordan smiled. "Yeah, I guess you have—in more ways than one. Okay, we'll do it your way."

McKenna walked ahead of them to unlock the door, grateful she didn't have the front porch she always wanted so there were no steps Mac would have to struggle with. She looked around the home she had so carefully created for herself. She walked from room to room, checking things out, and returned to the living room with a sigh of relief that everything seemed to be in order.

Mac was already settled into a recliner at one end of the sofa, and McKenna noticed her sister did look very tired and in pain.

"I'll get you some Tylenol," she said.

Jordan remained standing and didn't seem like he knew what he should do with himself. "Do you two need anything?" he asked as McKenna came back into the room.

"No, I don't think so," Mac said, taking the bottle of Tylenol.

McKenna said, "I'm sure there's little if anything to eat in the house, but I'll call out for dinner." She sensed Jordan's hesitancy about leaving. "Would you like to stay for dinner?"

"Thanks, but no," he said. "I think the two of you deserve some time alone for a while." He smiled. "But don't worry, Uncle Vernon will keep in touch."

"Thank you, Vernon, for everything," Mac said.

"You're welcome, Mac. I'm glad I could help and that things worked out the way they did."

McKenna walked him to the door. "Don't be a stranger, Uncle Vernon," she said with a smile. Then she returned to the living room and sat down on the sofa next to Mac. "Are you hungry? What do you want for dinner?"

"Oh, no, you don't," Mac said. "We're not talking about dinner yet. What's going on with you, Kenna? You seemed so quiet and kind of sad on the way to the safe house, but when you got back into the SUV, you were smiling from ear to ear. Spill it!"

"I think I'd like a glass of wine. How 'bout you?" McKenna asked as she headed for the kitchen for two wine glasses and a bottle of Cabernet Sauvignon.

"Sure," Mac said, "just make sure you come back in here."

McKenna returned and poured them each a glass of wine. She handed a glass to Mac and then took a sip of her own.

"Mac," she began tentatively, "have you ever dated a woman?"

Mac seemed surprised by the question but didn't hesitate to answer. "Yes, of course."

"Of course?" McKenna was puzzled. "What does that mean?"

"I guess I'm surprised that you didn't know. Do you remember my friend, Liz, from college?"

"Yeah," McKenna said. "I remember you were good friends for a couple of years. Why?"

"Yeah," Mac said with a smile. "You're right. We were *really* good friends,"

McKenna was shocked. "When you told me you were bisexual, I thought you were just telling me you were attracted to both women and men. I didn't know you had ever actually explored that in a relationship. Wow."

Mac put her hand over McKenna's hand. "This is about Nadia, right?"

McKenna nodded.

"I sensed there was something going on between the two of you," Mac said.

"But there really wasn't anything going on, Mac." She took another sip of wine. "I felt things when I was with Nadia that I've never felt before. I've never had those feelings with a man or a woman."

"What about Zack?" Mac asked, referring to McKenna's short marriage.

"No," McKenna said. "We were friends, yes, and we thought we could be more than friends, but it just never felt right—not to either one of us, I think."

"So have you said anything to Nadia about how you feel?"

"No, no way," McKenna insisted. "I couldn't make sense of my own feelings. Even if I had, I would have been embarrassed if I told her, and she didn't feel that way about me."

Mac smiled. "Oh, I think you're not alone in your feelings, Kenna. When the two of you were together in my hospital room, the energy between you could have powered a small town."

It was McKenna's turn to smile. "Really? You could feel that, too? Wow." She took the piece of paper out of her shirt pocket. "I thought it was just me until I found this in my shirt pocket." She handed the note to Mac, who read it, smiled, and handed it back.

"So as bad as all of this has been, there have been some good things come out of it all," Mac said. "We have an uncle we never knew we had. The president of the United States feels a connection to us. And you have experienced a part of yourself you've never known before." She smiled. "Wow is right. That's a lot to happen in just a few days. You *are* going to call her, right?"

"Yes! I want to. I plan to, but I don't know how to be with her, Mac."

"Just be yourself, Kenna. That's who she's attracted to. The rest will come to you along the way."

# Chapter 35

The next day, true to his word, Jordan had gotten someone to locate McKenna's car and return it to her home. As they went to get into her car, McKenna noticed Mac walking without the crutches, limping just a little but doing pretty well.

"Are you supposed to be doing that?" she asked with a frown.

"They told me the bullet went through and through. My leg is not broken. They told me to be gentle with it for a few days—as in, no hiking, running, or crossing that leg. Other than that, just take the antibiotic and use my own judgment based on how I feel. I'm using my own judgment. I don't need those things."

McKenna shook her head and sighed. "Okay, well, you know your body."

When they arrived at Mac's apartment complex, McKenna parked the car, and they both walked to her door. Mac hesitated before unlocking it.

"What's wrong?" McKenna asked, concerned.

"I just didn't expect to feel like this," Mac said with a frown. "The last time I opened this door was when I met David here. I was armed. He was armed. I feel as anxious now as I did that night." She turned to McKenna. "I wonder if I'm going to be able to live here again, Kenna."

McKenna put her arm around her sister. "I get it. Maybe you will and maybe you won't. Let's get inside and give yourself some time."

\* \* \*

Mac opened the door and took a tentative step inside. Her apartment looked just as it did when she and David left that night. The chairs they sat in as they talked were in the same position. Her horn was lying on the chair that he had been sitting in. There was no mouthpiece on it, though. The mouthpiece was his, and he must have taken it with him.

She slowly walked through each room, wondering how much of her privacy he had violated. Did he look through her drawers? Did he read her journal? And even as she asked herself those questions, she knew she would never have answers.

She looked at the various kinds of horns on her walls, bookcases, and tables. She touched some of them gently as she moved through each room. She remembered him telling her that he had once collected horns the way she did, and that he even had many of the same kinds of things—except for her poster of the Horn of Plenty.

He had commented on that one, saying, "I turned something I loved into a Horn of Plenty of a different kind. I used it to make money—a lot of money."

She thought about all the things David told her that night, and she remembered that, even though she knew he had tried to kill her—or have her killed—several times, she had surprised herself by feeling compassion for the lonely boy he had been. She could almost understand how that lonely boy had become a lonely, twisted man. He also spoke about loving the French Horn in a way that echoed so many of her own thoughts and feelings. It was hard not to feel conflicted about him. Then there was the trust he'd left for Ann Headley's children.

David had done a lot of bad things—criminal things—but there must have been some good left in him. He turned his illegal earnings over to the government and turned his legal earnings into a trust for two motherless children. He had refused to participate in a terrorist attack and swore he loved his country. Did he find redemption in those final choices he made? That was another question for which she would never have an answer.

McKenna interrupted her thoughts. "Mac? Are you okay?"

Mac wiped a few tears from her eyes. Was she crying for David? For all the people who had died through all of this? For her parents? For herself? She wasn't sure, but at the moment, it didn't matter.

"No, not yet, Kenna, but I'm going to be."

\* \* \*

The following day, Mac called Captain Jamison so she could hear directly from him what her status was. As she anticipated, his aide and her friend, Jennifer, answered and told her the captain was not available.

"However," Jennifer told her, "He expected that you might be calling and asked if you would come by his office on Monday at 1000. Can you do that?"

"Yeah, sure," Mac said, "I'll be there."

She ended the call, but it stayed in her mind. She was trying to read the tone of Jennifer's voice to give her some idea of what awaited her, but she found herself without a clue. She didn't ask Mac any questions, and she didn't let any scuttlebutt slip, if there was any. President Holton had assured her everything would be okay, but Mac still found it hard to believe.

She started to put her phone down then decided to call McKenna. She needed a ride to pick up a rental car until she could shop for a new one, and she had to be able to get to the Navy Yard on Monday morning.

* * *

Mac spent the weekend working to get back into a regular routine. In spite of the soreness that remained in her ribs and leg and the bruises that had now bloomed into a strange blend of yellow and purple all over her body, she did some light cleaning, cleaned out her refrigerator, bought groceries, and played her horn. However, she now found playing her horn to be a little bittersweet. She still loved it as she always had but playing reminded her of what she had given up, of David, and of all that had happened, not only to her and McKenna, but also to her parents. She listened to mournful pieces of music that helped her cry because she had some innate sense that her body needed to cry, to mourn. It did—and it helped.

When she left for the Navy Yard Monday morning, she felt ready to face whatever would happen, even if it meant having to start all over again. She arrived at Captain Jamison's office at 0930.

Jennifer was horrified when she saw her. "Oh, my God, Mac! Are you okay?!"

"Yeah, Jen," she said sheepishly. "You should see the other guy."

Jennifer smiled and came out from behind her desk to give Mac a gentle hug. "He should be with you shortly."

Mac felt like it was less painful for her to remain standing than to sit down and have to stand back up again in a short space of time. She was glad she made that choice when Jamison walked into his office.

He smiled but was clearly shocked by her appearance. "It's good to see you, Mac, but are you sure you feel up to being here?"

"Yes, sir," she said. "This is exactly where I want to be."

Jamison nodded. "Very good, then. Walk with me."

She followed him from his office and down the long corridor toward the rehearsal room. "I didn't bring my horn with me today, sir."

"That's okay. You won't be needing it."

They reached the end of the corridor, and he opened the door to the rehearsal room for Mac to enter. When she did, she gasped. The entire Navy Concert Band was assembled but without instruments. There was one empty seat in the horn section—at the very end of the row. She stood speechless as Jamison went to his podium and turned toward her.

"Chief Musician Hollingsworth. Few of us in any of the Navy Bands are likely to find ourselves in harm's way. We understand that you have—and that is evident by the looks of you here today. We also understand that the special assignment you were on involved classified information vital to national security. All of us—including me—have been ordered not to question you about this assignment or any of the facts surrounding it. We understand that you are unable to answer such questions." He paused for a moment then motioned to one of the horn players. "Katrina has done a wonderful job serving as Acting Principal Horn in your absence, and her service has been noted. However, we're all here today to welcome you home, Mac. Whatever the hell you did, well done."

The entire band stood and began to applaud. The entire horn section shifted down a seat, leaving the Principal Chair open. Mac was overwhelmed, and tears rolled down her cheeks in spite of her best efforts to hold them back. Jamison stepped down from the podium and walked toward her and held out his hand to shake hers.

"Thank you, sir. Thank you, Katrina. Thank you, everyone. It's good to be back."

\* \* \*

After the surprising welcome-back meeting, many of her friends in the band welcomed her back individually. No one asked forbidden questions, but Mac could sense they were curious, especially knowing she had been injured. They set aside their curiosity, however, and seemed genuinely grateful that whatever this special mission was, she was back and would fully recover soon. Mac and Jamison agreed she needed a little more time to recover and would resume her position the following week.

Mac returned to her apartment around noon. Once again, as she unlocked the door, she remembered that night with David.

*How long will it take for me to feel normal when I'm unlocking my door?*

She slowly and painfully took off her uniform and put on the softest, most comfortable sweats she owned. She hung her uniform in the closet and then leaned against the closet door frame and stared at the uniform she had worn with such pride for fifteen years. She closed her eyes and remembered how painful it had been to feel like she might have to give up a career that was so integral to who she was. A single tear ran down her cheek, and she brushed it away as she closed the closet door.

She went into the living room, and scenes from that night began to replay in her head.

*Here we go again.*

She went to the kitchen to get a bottle of water from the refrigerator and surprised herself by thinking about getting a new dry-erase board. She laughed out loud at having such a mundane thought after feeling inundated by scenes from that night here with David.

She started toward the living room but stopped in the dining room she used as her practice area. She picked up her horn case, then went back into the living room and settled on the sofa. She took her horn out, pressed each key, and tested the movement of each slide.

*They need a little slide grease*, she thought.

She didn't laugh out loud this time, but she did smile as she realized that she must be easing into some kind of new normal for her thoughts to move from those recent traumatic events to thoughts of normal, everyday things.

She turned her head toward the dining room and looked at the poster of the Horn of Plenty. She remembered David's words about it and how sad he had seemed.

*No*, she thought, *sad isn't the right word.*

She wasn't sure what the right word was, though. The emotions she saw in him seemed deeper than sadness. Whatever feelings he exhibited that night, she was grateful she had never experienced them—and hoped she never would. In spite of all he had done, she hoped his actions at the end had brought him some sense of redemption or peace.

She looked at the poster again, then closed her eyes. She felt a wave of warmth move through her as she realized that her life as it had been—and now would be again—was in so many ways a Horn of Plenty for her.

## ABOUT THE AUTHOR

Martha Jane Hovater is both the birthname and pen name for the author of *Horn of Plenty*. She's been a writer and avid reader since childhood but only recently gave her writing the attention needed to complete her first novel. Having done that, she has finally figured out how to juggle "real life" demands and her desire to write and is excited to see where her writing may take her.

Martha lives in Maryland with her partner of 33 years (Barbara), one of their daughters (JoAnn), a canine furbaby (Zack), and a canine granddog (Ninja).

*Horn of Plenty* is her first published novel.

https://marthajanehovater.com/
https://www.facebook.com/marthajanehovater.author